AiRi 💀 SANO
PRANKMASTER GENERAL
★ ★ ★

New School Skirmish

AiRi SANO PRANKMASTER GENERAL

★ ★ ★

New School Skirmish

Written by **ZOE TOKUSHIGE**

Illustrations by
JENNIFER NAALCHIGAR

PHILOMEL BOOKS

For my teachers Scott Waxler and Shannon Vaughan,
who believed in my writing before anyone else

PHILOMEL BOOKS
An imprint of Penguin Random House LLC, New York

First published in the United States of America by Philomel Books,
an imprint of Penguin Random House LLC, 2022

Copyright © 2022 by Cake Creative LLC

cakecreativekitchen.com

Philomel Books is a registered trademark of Penguin Random House LLC.

Visit us online at penguinrandomhouse.com.

Library of Congress Cataloging-in-Publication Data is available.

Printed in the United States of America

ISBN 9780593465783

1st Printing

LSCH

Edited by Talia Benamy

Design by Monique Sterling

Text set in Jazmin

AIRI SANO'S CASE FILE

The US Army has a file on me at least five hundred pages thick. An OMPF.[1] That's what Mom says, anyway. She says we ought to request it so I can "learn the effects of my behavior" and "start to think before I act." She always sighs when she says that. Then she looks up at the ceiling and asks, "How did I raise such a delinquent?"

I like it better when she gets mad. Her face gets all red like a pepper, and she uses my full name: "Airi. Evelyn. Sano." Like that. You can *hear* the periods. It always makes me giggle. When she sighs, there's nothing to laugh at.

I had to look up the word "delinquent" online when she first used it. There were a few definitions. Here are my favorites:

---

1 That stands for Official Military Personnel File. The army uses all kinds of abbreviations and acronyms. Dad says there are over 1,000! I used to think it was silly when they could use normal words, but it's fun to make up new ones. Like OMDB. That's Over My Dead Body, which is what I tell E.J. when he asks to use my iPod.

delinquent (de-LING-kwent)

1. *noun*—a usually young person who regularly performs illegal or immoral acts

2. *adjective*—neglectful of a duty or obligation; guilty of a misdeed or offense

Synonyms: offender, wrongdoer, malefactor, lawbreaker, culprit, criminal

I also found a bunch of mug shots. Turns out that means pictures of criminals, not actual mugs. At first I thought "mug" stood for something, like MUG: Mostly Unwashed Guy. Then I remembered back when Dad was stationed at Fort Mackall-Bragg in Fayetteville, North Carolina, I heard one of my teachers say a kid had "a mug only a mother could love" after he broke his nose falling off the jungle gym. I asked Dad about it later and he said "mug" is an old-fashioned way of saying "face," but he didn't know why. I didn't get it then, and I don't get it now.

These days, when Mom calls me a delinquent, I leave little drawings of what my mug shot might look like—if I ever actually get arrested—all over the house for her. I even asked my obaachan (that's what I call my grandma in Japan) how to write "delinquent" in kanji (不良少女[2]) to

---

2 It's spelled something like "furyou shoujo" if you want to write it in English. You say it fhoo-dYO SHO-jo. Mom's English is practically perfect (that's what everyone says), but she likes it when I use Japanese.

really make my point. I like to hide the pictures so she'll find them when she least expects it. Sometimes I'll be across the house and I'll hear her yelp when she opens the bathroom cabinet and sees me smirking back.

"Smirking" means "to smile in an insincere manner." A teacher once accused me of smirking and gave me a demerit. When I said I didn't even know what a smirk was, she gave me a second demerit and a note to give my parents. Mom sighed extra loud that day.

I started drawing the mug shots because I thought they were funny. I hoped they would make Mom laugh. Dad likes them. He collects them all for my file and compliments me on the different faces. But Mom never laughs. Which is the whole point.

What I'm saying is that she thinks I'm bad. Everyone thinks I'm bad. People just don't have a sense of humor. They don't get it. That's why I started my own case file. An Official Personal Personnel File (aka an OPPF). If the army is going to keep a report on me, I want to tell my side of the story too.

Now when I get put out in the hall or sent to the vice principal's office, I'll be documenting it. Then the next time I get called in for a "talk" on why I'm not "fitting in," I won't have to say a word. All I'll have to do is give them my file. This portfolio of information, all for them to see. Just like the ones that Dad brings home sometimes, the ones that aren't classified. That way when Mom or my teacher or anyone asks, "What were you thinking, Airi?" I'll be able to show them this.

And if you still think I'm bad, then fine. If this is bad, then I'll be bad. I'll be the happiest, baddest delinquent you've ever seen.

PERSONNEL FILE

Name
Sano, Airi (SAW-no, EYE-ree)[3]

Date of Birth
April 7

Place of Birth
Sagamihara, Japan

Place of Residence
Fort Shafter, Hawai'i

Formerly Fayetteville, North Carolina; Hopkinsville, Kentucky; Burlington, New Jersey; Fairfax, Virginia; San Antonio, Texas; Pine Bluff, Arkansas. Also a little time in South Korea, but I was too young to remember that.

Occupation
Delinquent

Primary Specialties
Causing trouble, making people laugh, pranks

Awards and Citations
Most Disruptive Student, Best Baby Soother (according to Dad), Genius Prankster

Disciplinary Record
Too long to include full list

Remarks
Dad keeps promising I can take fighting classes when we find a place for me to go, but it hasn't happened yet. By the end of next year, I want to add Karate Master to my specialties.

---

3   EYE-ree is the easiest way for Americans to say it. Actually, "r"s in Japanese sound almost like "d"s. Your tongue has to touch the top of your mouth to do it right.

SITUATION REPORT

Date
Friday, September 3

Location
Fort Shafter, Hawai'i

Activities Planned
Finish moving into our new house

Logistical Requirements
Scissors (to open the boxes)

Step stool (to put things up in the cabinets)

Obstacles Anticipated
Dad is at work, so no one can reach the highest shelves.

Remarks
Dad set up a lot of stuff before we got here! It was nice to come into a new house and for once not have to sleep on the floor the first night.

THE PHONE iN OuR NEW HOUSE RiNGS AND RiNGS AND rings. We've only been on base for twenty-four hours, so how does anyone even know we're home? We haven't had the chance to visit Grandma and Grandpa yet. They don't even know we've arrived. Dad wants to surprise them.

Mom is busy strapping my little sister into her high chair, so I push myself up onto the kitchen counter to grab the phone. Mom tells me to get down, but Kaori distracts her by trying to climb out of her seat. Kaori's my favorite. She always distracts Mom at just the right moment.

"*Yellow?*" I say into the phone.

"Excuse me? Hello?" says the voice on the other end. I don't recognize it, and they don't have a local accent, which means they aren't family. I smile to myself. That makes it more fun.

"*Yellow*," I say again. "*Orange* you glad you got me?"

"I'm calling for Lieutenant Colonel Sano," the voice says, completely ignoring my jokes. "Could you put him on the line?"

"I'll *teal* him you called," I say. Teal is my favorite color. "*Blue* are you?"

The voice gets all tense and annoyed now. "Is one of your parents home?" I can just tell he's gritting his teeth.

I'm trying to think of another color to use when Mom snatches the phone from my hand. She apologizes to the man on the other end and asks him to hold on for a moment. That means I'm in trouble.

Sure enough, she puts her hand over the mouthpiece and frowns at me.

"Airi, I thought we agreed you were going to try harder to behave once we moved here," she whispers. "You said you wouldn't make trouble anymore."

I want to tell her that I never signed anything—Dad says that's what makes an agreement official—but she's already talking on the phone again. She takes the caller's name and a message and hangs up. Then she crosses her arms and looks at me. Usually that means she's about to lecture me about being more respectful.

"I said I would be *nicer*," I protest before she can say anything. "I've been *very* nice."

And I have!

1. I sorted the recycling without being asked. I even rinsed out the bottles and cans like Mom likes so that we wouldn't get ants.

2. I changed Kaori's diaper while Mom was busy with the cable people and played with her so she wouldn't crawl away and stick her finger in a socket. Not that Kaori would actually do that, but grown-ups seem to think that's the first thing any baby wants to do.

3. I organized the shoes on our front step so we wouldn't trip on them when we went out. We don't have a little shelf in the entryway like we used to because Dad doesn't want us getting mud in the house.[4]

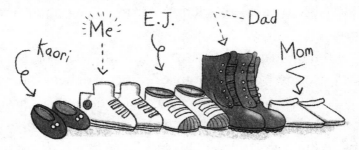

Kaori   Me   E.J.   Dad   Mom

Mom shakes her head. "You promised that when we got to Hawai'i, things would be different. You'd be more mature. But this is something the old Airi would have done."

I look down at the ugly brown tiles instead of her disappointed face. My stomach is all queasy. It seems like Mom's been giving me more and more of those disappointed looks these days. Even though I'm the same me I've always been.

Mom gives one of her big sighs. "Do you have anything to say?"

---

4 We never wear shoes in the house. We have house slippers for when it's cold, but usually I just run around in my socks. It's easier to slide around.

That means she wants me to apologize.

"Oh my *god*," I say. "It was a joke! Most people think it's funny." Actually, only Grandma laughs at my yellow joke. But if more people were like her, they'd think it was funny too. "Orange you tickled pink?" I give Mom a big smile so she'll know I'm joking around.

"Go to your room," Mom says. She isn't smiling even a little. I open my mouth to protest—I didn't *mean* any harm— but Kaori starts crying just then, like she can sense Mom's mood. Mom turns to soothe her, forgetting about me. I sprint off.

I run past my little brother, E.J., who's watching TV quietly like a good, respectful child. Past the cat bed where Mr. Knuckles will sleep once he's out of pet quarantine. Through the trail of Cheerios Kaori left on her way to the kitchen. Up, up, up the stairs to the only place I like in this new house. My room.

Two teal walls and two red—that's my other favorite color—even though Mom said they don't match. My base-ball cards, which used to be my grandpa's, framed on the wall. My stacks of comic books. And even though my room has a bunk bed, I don't have to share it. I can use it to make a fort or a secret hideaway where I can plan my next mission.

When Dad told me we were moving again, this was part of our agreement. I wouldn't have to share with E.J. any-more. I'd get a place that was just mine. I could fill it with as much junk as I wanted, because this time we were staying. No more moving. He even let me draw him a diagram of

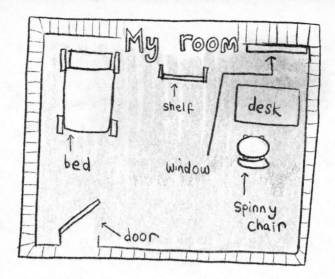

how I wanted everything set up, and he copied it perfectly, just for me. Because he does things like that.

Dad put a desk next to the window, which looks out into our new backyard. I sit in the spinny chair that used to be his and spread out my collection of report cards. I've been turning them into a collage. Cutting them up neatly to glue along a piece of thick paper. A lovely pattern of Cs and Ds, surrounded by a halo of my teachers' comments. The Great Airi Sano.

Fifth-Grade Report Card

Student: Airi Sano	Fourth-Quarter Grades
ELA:	D
Reading:	D
Science:	D
Social Studies:	C-
Math:	D
Art:	A-
PE:	C

"*Airi could benefit from more attention to detail in her work, and an attitude adjustment to make her participation in class more productive and less distracting to other students.*" —Mrs. Parekh

"*While spirited, Airi's pranks are rarely amusing, especially when directed at her teachers, and they are frequently disruptive to class.*" —Mr. Simmons

"*Although Airi occasionally has difficulty following instructions, she is always eager to try new things and is an enthusiastic and talented young artist. I'd like to see her collaborate more with other students.*" —Ms. Meyers

"*Airi was a keen participator in our science labs, particularly when it came to making explosions. I'd love to see her give as much attention and excitement to her notes, quizzes, and classwork.*" —Ms. Evanson

Grown-ups say that school is important because it helps you decide what you want to do with your life. I think maybe some kids need that, because they don't know anything. They think they want to be doctors or accountants or whatever their parents do. I know I don't want to be in the army (too many rules), and I know I don't want to be a travel agent like Mom was (boring). I'm already perfectly happy the way I am. School just holds me back.

THINGS I COULD DO WITH MY LIFE
IF I DIDN'T HAVE TO GO TO SCHOOL

- ⭐ YouTube prankster, though I think most of those people fake it

- ⭐ Pirate, because pirates do still exist no matter what E.J. says

- ⭐ Comic artist (people just make their own and put them online)

- ⭐ Deep-sea explorer—I'm not afraid of small spaces *or* the ocean

- ⭐ Pop star, which doesn't really seem very fun, but you don't have to go to school for it

- ⭐ Superhero, but one without superpowers, like Batgirl or Elektra (I need the karate lessons that Dad promised, but that's not like school)

- ⭐ Olympic athlete (see above about karate)

- ⭐ Pet sitter, preferably cats

Dad says my new school is supposed to be good. It isn't a base school, it's a normal public school, which means it isn't just military kids. I like base schools. Other military kids know the score. We all keep our distance, because we know we might move any day. Normal kids want to be friends. And I've tried that. But those friendships never last.

The other thing about base schools is that there are usually more kinds of people. But in places like Kentucky, where I went to a public school, E.J. and I were the only Asian kids.

Which can get old. People always had the most ridiculous questions. Like:

"Why don't you wear a kimono?"

"Can you teach me karate?"

"Are you secretly a ninja?"

"Do you really eat raw fish? That's so gross!"

"Does your dad use a katana when he fights?"

"What's your favorite anime?"

I actually have an answer for that last one, but usually the person asking just wants to tell me why the anime they like is better. E.J. and I like *One Piece*. It's just about the only thing that we can agree on.

Here, though, there are way more Asian people. I know Mom used to like it when we visited, because when we went to the mall we'd hear all the Japanese tourists talking, and it would remind her of home. And there aren't just Japanese people here. Dad's best friend, Uncle Dan, is Korean, and my grandparents' neighbors are Filipino. So people aren't going to think weird things just because my last name is Sano.

But even if the kids at this school are less annoying—and even if they might want to be friends with me—there's one major thing I already hate about this school.

I'm starting sixth grade. Everywhere else, that means middle school. Not here. I still have to be in elementary school with all the babies. And E.J. That's the worst part. Being in the same school as E.J. means all the teachers know both of us. They always want to know why I can't be more like him. I hate being compared to E.J. He's good at school. He even likes it.

Mom and Dad keep telling me I'm going to have to try harder this time. Get better grades. Like I haven't tried before. But the results are always the same whether I try or not, so I might as well have fun. I just have to get my teacher on board. Which means I need to make them realize as soon as possible that I'm unteachable. No wasting time trying to "reach" me or be my friend. Because they'll only be disappointed later.

By now I've perfected the art of Teacher Tactics. It won't take long before they write me off as the "problem kid," and then it'll be smooth sailing. That's how you survive school when you're a delinquent. You aren't the new kid, or the Asian kid, or the bad student. You're the lost cause. The one they leave alone. And that's how I like it.

PERSONNEL FILE

Name
Sano, Reiko (RAY-koh[5]);
maiden name Nakano
(Nah-CAH-no)

Date of Birth
December 22

Place of Birth
Osaka, Japan

Place of Residence
Fort Shafter, Hawai'i

Formerly Fayetteville, North
Carolina, plus everywhere
else I've lived, and also
Innoshima (ee-NO-shee-mah)
Island, Japan, and Tokyo,
Japan

Occupation
Mom

Formerly travel agent

Primary Specialties
Cooking, finding deals, the
Disappointed Look

Awards and Citations
Most Polite Ever, Best
Football Sushi

Disciplinary Record
Doesn't get my jokes most
of the time. Once, she forgot
to tip our waitress, but she
went back the next day and
gave her extra.

Remarks
"Respectful" is one of Mom's
favorite words. She also
likes "dutiful" and "helpful."
All of which I'm not. She
says I'm too old now to be
so "irresponsible." I don't
see why getting older
means I have to change my
whole personality.

Mom used to spend a lot
of time with me and E.J.
helping with homework and
trying to teach us Japanese.
Since Kaori was born, she's
had way less time. She's
always running after Kaori,
and it makes her really tired.
And she's sick of moving
around. I heard her and Dad
arguing about it before we
left North Carolina. That's
why Hawai'i is supposed to
be permanent.

---

5 See Personnel Report on Airi Sano (aka me) about how to correctly
pronounce the "r" sound.

PERSONNEL FILE

Name
Sano, Eiji (AY-jee), aka E.J.

Date of Birth
July 11

Place of Birth
Seoul, South Korea

Place of Residence
Fort Shafter, Hawai'i

Formerly Fayetteville, North Carolina, and everywhere else I've lived

Occupation
Little brother, know-it-all

Primary Specialties
Getting perfect grades, playing *Minecraft*

Awards and Citations
Honor Student, Class Monitor, Most Frequent Winner of the Right to Decide What Movie We're Watching

Disciplinary Record
Once got put in time-out for putting gum in my hair (age five). He's never been any fun since then.

Remarks
He started going by E.J. because people couldn't say his name right. I think he should have made people learn to say it right.

Surefire way to annoy him is to play "Baby Shark." When we shared a room back in North Carolina, I set Dad's old iPod to play that through our alarm every morning, even though I hate it too. But E.J. hated it more. And every time he tried to change it, I'd change it back.

SITUATION REPORT

Date
Sunday, September 5

Location
Fort Shafter, Hawai'i

Activities Planned
Neighborhood reconnaissance[6]

Welcome barbecue

Logistical Requirements
Halloween costume (nightgown, ketchup, oil, flour)

Bike

Obstacles Anticipated
I need to get out of the house before Mom sees me.

E.J. might tell on me.

Remarks
These welcome barbecues are always so boring. This time I'm going to make it a little more fun.

---

6 Pronounced ree-CAW-nah-sawnce. Dad uses this word a lot. It means looking around an area to learn about things you can use and to learn about the enemy. The enemy in this case being our new neighbors.

My Guide to O'ahu, Hawai'i

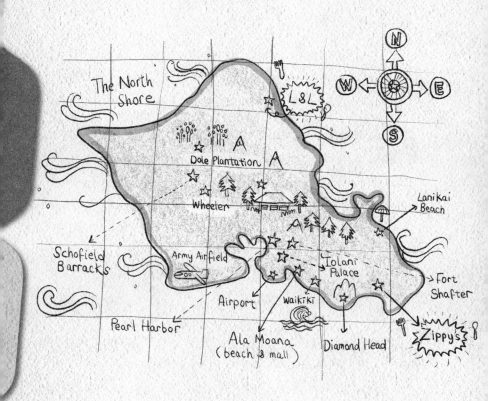

IT'S SUNDAY. WE'VE BEEN HERE FOR SEVENTY-TWO hours, which means it's time to survey the neighborhood. I would have done it yesterday, except we went to visit Grandma and Grandpa on the other side of the island instead. They live on a Christmas tree farm that has tons of wild chickens. My cousin Noah and I spent most of the afternoon trying to catch one, but they're a lot faster than you'd think.

Noah is my favorite cousin. He's E.J.'s age—one year younger than me—but he's much more fun than E.J. He showed me how to do a crane kick last time we spent Thanksgiving in Hawai'i (his parents let him take fighting classes). Grandpa likes to complain that we're noisy, but when Grandma was in the kitchen, he gave us some tips on catching the chickens.

It was a big party, the kind I like because people are loud and friendly and there's lots of food. Dad's family has the best parties. Dad made huli huli chicken on the grill, and Uncle Dan brought fresh poke that he made from fish he caught himself. All my aunties and uncles gave us leis, especially Dad. He had so many on they almost covered his whole face. Kaori immediately got into one of the big puddles that are always around the farm and got absolutely *covered* in mud. It was perfect.

Poke (poh-kay): You probably think you know poke because it's popular on the mainland, but that isn't *real* poke. That stuff is like a sushi bowl. Real poke is raw fish that's all cut up and marinated with soy sauce, seaweed, sesame oil, and a little chili. It's usually made from tuna, but there's also salmon and octopus poke. When we visited before, we'd go to Costco and get a big batch and eat it with fresh hot rice for lunch. It's so good.

Today we're supposed to have another party, which I already know isn't going to be nearly as fun. Every time we move to a new base there's some kind of party with the neighbors. I always have to be on my best behavior, and all the adults stand around talking about work and boring things like that.

The good thing is that I have my Halloween costume ready, even though it's still almost two months until Halloween (which is *really* called All Hallows' Eve, but everyone says Halloween now, so I go along with it—even if it is *NOT* correct—so people know what I'm talking about). That means I can have a little fun.

First, I use oil to get my hair nice and greasy. Then I powder my skin with enough flour to make an okonomiyaki. I even drip some ketchup on my face and clothes so that it looks like fake blood. When I peek in the bathroom mirror, I look just like the evil little girl from the movie Mom and Dad watched last Halloween (**cough** All Hallows' Eve) after they put me and E.J. to bed. I snuck back out and watched from the staircase until the commercial break. Then I jumped out and yelled, "Ahh!"

mayo
toppings
pork
sauce
cabbage

Okonomiyaki (oh-KOH-no-mee-YAH-kee): This is a tasty pancake, but it isn't sweet, and you can add all kinds of stuff to it—meat, yams, even rice cakes and kimchi. Then you put this sweet-salty sauce and mayo on top, and you cover it in toppings—tempura flakes, seaweed, little shrimp, fish flakes. Fish flakes are fun because they wiggle in the air. They make your food look like it's moving.

Mom screamed.

I laughed.

Dad clutched at his chest and said a bad word.

My punishment was that I had to give away all the candy I'd gotten while trick-or-treating to my teachers. I tried to hide some in my room, but Mom knew all my hiding places in our old house. I'm working on making better ones this time.

At least it meant my teachers went easy on me for a few days. "Bribery will get you everywhere," Mr. Simmons said. He took all the Milky Ways.

Mom is in the living room playing with Kaori, so I sneak past into the kitchen. E.J. is in there with a book like a big nerd. I don't get what the big deal is with books like the ones he likes. They don't even have cool illustrations, just pages and pages of boring words. His eyes widen when he sees me. I put my finger to my lips and then drag it across my neck like I've seen bad guys in movies do. He rolls his eyes but doesn't tell on me.

The sliding glass door is a lot louder than I thought it would be, and Mom calls, "Airi? Is that you?"

E.J. looks at me. I know better than to think he'll lie for me, so I yell, "Just going for a bike ride!"

"Be back before the barbecue! Dad will be home in an hour."

"Okay. Where is it?"

"Just out on the block. So nice of them to throw a party for us, isn't it?"

"Yep!" I say. She says this every time we move to a new base.

"Are you wearing your ID?"

"Yep," I say again. I have it tucked into the collar of my white dress so that it doesn't ruin the costume. Mom would scold me if she saw, but no one is going to ask for it. No one ever does. I take a step out the door.

"And take E.J. with you," Mom calls. E.J. makes a face. I make a face back.

"It's okay," E.J. says. "I'll wait to go with you and Dad."

I give him a thumbs-up. Sometimes the two of us do think alike.

"Did you put on the dress we got?"

"Of course!" I lie.

"Let me see." Her footsteps start to approach the kitchen. Then there's a big crash and Kaori starts wailing. She really does have such great timing for knowing when to distract Mom. It's like we have a sister sense. Mom's footsteps retreat.

"Mom's gonna kill you," E.J. tells me.

"Not right now," I say, and I scurry out the door before Mom finishes with Kaori.

I sneak around to the front of the house to get my bike. The garage is big enough to fit almost three cars, so E.J. and I have room to store our bikes. We used to have to leave them outside. Our bikes have traveled all over with us. They practically deserve frequent-flier status.

My bike is turtle green with a sloped seat. I've taped my

favorite playing cards—the jacks from Dad's old Star Wars deck—to the spokes. There's a bell on the handlebars and a string of tin cans attached to the back. I got the idea from a wedding we went to. They drag along behind me and rumble like a little storm cloud. I love that sound. If people had signature sounds the way Aunty Jen says celebrities have signature perfumes, that would be mine.

I set out down the driveway. The air is hot and wet, like being slapped with a damp towel. Grandma always tells me to wear a hat or a visor to protect my eyes, but it wouldn't match my outfit. I start sweating. It's making the flour clump. It's going to ruin my whole look.

Once I start really going, though, there's enough breeze to cool me off. I look left and right. One thing I have to say about this base is that at least it doesn't all look the same. One time in Kentucky right after we moved, Mom got confused and pulled into the wrong house. We were trying to get the door open when the woman who lived there opened it up. Mom was so embarrassed. I thought it was pretty funny.

We live in one of the bigger houses here because Dad's an important person. People always tell me how lucky I am to have such a hardworking dad. I'd be okay if he worked a little less, even if it meant we lived in one of the smaller places like the ones I pass on Ala Amoamo. I yell the street name as I pass. AH-la Ah-mo-AH-mo. Dad taught me how to say it. I like how it feels in my mouth.

I squeeze the horn on my bike. I've decided I like announcing myself. It will come in handy. Dad says that sometimes there are big sirens here to let you know about a tsunami. Mom says I'm a force of nature too, so it seems only fair to let people know I'm coming. It'll keep the rest of the base safe.

I turn the corner onto the next street, Ala Kolopua. I pass an oldish lady watering her big orange flowers. She yells, "Can't you keep it down?" as I pass.

"What did you say?" I shout. "I can't hear you!" I ride away as quickly as possible, swirling in figure eights before turning down the next street.

The blocks here are long, and the streets are way curvier than I'm used to. I'm gonna have to make a map of this base. Most of the others I could have memorized in a few weeks, but things here aren't laid out in neat rows like I'm used to. I kind of like it. It feels almost like living in a real neighborhood, one with houses that look all different with big backyards and funny gnomes on the lawn.

I bike past a group of soldiers jogging in straight lines. They're all wearing camo fatigues, which looks like it must be hot. The leader at the front of the lines yells:

"LEFT, RIGHT, LEFT. LEFT, RIGHT, LEFT."

I try to keep up with them. One waves me off like I'm a fly. A couple smile before looking serious again. I follow so close that the one at the end turns and gives me one of those scary soldier death glares. I salute him to let him know that he's won this round. But it won't be the last he sees of me.

I watch them run away. Perfect lines. Identical uniforms. Nearly bald heads. Lots of chanting. I think of my dad leading them, or even my grandpa. Grandpa was in the army, and my great-grandpa too. Dad is very proud of it. I'm proud too, mostly when I get to see them dressed up in their fancy uniforms. It's about the only thing I like about the military. They get dressed in their blue suits with their buttons shining like bright new pennies, with lots of medals and badges to show that they're important.

Dad keeps my great-grandpa's medals in a case up-stairs. He explained them to me once. The one I remember best is the Purple Heart, which you get if you're wounded in action.

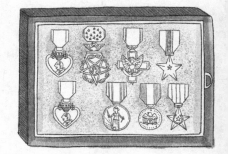

Great-Grandpa had *two*. Dad says he got one in France and one in Italy. He says it's our duty to make Great-Grandpa proud.

I turn down Ala Mahamoe to loop back toward the house. When I start getting closer to Palm Circle Drive, I start passing people who must be going to the barbecue too. They hold hamburger buns and overflowing grocery bags. Some have big coolers they drag behind them. One has a bunch of cans stacked in a little red wagon. The cans have brightly colored labels, which probably means they're soda or juice. My favorite. There's a little girl about Kaori's age sitting next to them. She waves, and I wave back.

As I get closer, I hear the people talking about the barbecue. Some of them notice me pass. Their eyebrows lift. A few laugh, which I love.

The sound of laughter is the best thing in the world. I love hearing all kinds of laughs:

Light, giggly ones like Kaori's that sound like little tinkling bells.

The type that turn into coughs.

Ones where people laugh so hard they start to cry.

The snicker Mom tries to swallow down to pretend that she isn't the kind of person who laughs.

The kind that get stuck in your nose, like E.J.'s, and spill out into donkey snorts.

The horsey ones that surprise everyone.

The deep, rumbling chuckle that makes Dad close his eyes.

If I could hear only one thing forever, it would be laughter.

I speed ahead of the crowd to get to my house before they do. Some kids around E.J.'s age chase after my bike, but I'm too fast for them. The street in front of our house is decked out: smoking grills, a big bouncy castle, tables of cupcakes and cookies, and a swarm of kids. I zip up the driveway and park my bike next to Dad's car.

E.J. is standing just inside the garage like he's afraid to go out where people are. He crosses his arms when he sees me.

"Are you going to change?" he asks.

"Nope," I say.

"What are you even supposed to be?"

"What does it look like?"

E.J. pushes up his glasses. "It looks weird, Airi."

E.J. likes to act like he's older than me. It's really annoying. He might be better at school than me, but I'm more fun, and I know how things work. He's a big scaredy-cat. He follows all the rules and never disobeys Mom and Dad, which makes him dead boring.

"You just don't understand my genius," I tell him. He snorts before inching out of the garage. "Where are Mom and Dad?"

E.J. points to the porch, where Mom, Dad, and Kaori have just come out. Kaori is squirming like she wants to escape Mom's arms. Dad is looking around for us. I duck inside and say, "Close the garage door."

"What?"

"I'm going to surprise them," I say. E.J. shakes his head but reaches into his pocket for the button that controls the garage door. He hasn't let anyone else use the button since we got here.

E.J. follows me back into the house. I creep up to the front door, peering out the window to see where Mom and Dad are. Mom has put Kaori down on the grass with some other babies. Good. I grab E.J. and shove him toward the door.

"You go first," I say.

"You're going to get in so much trouble," E.J. says, but he does what I say. I think he secretly likes it when I do things like this. It's probably the only fun he ever has.

E.J. opens the door and goes outside to join our parents. Dad and Mom smile and start introducing him to people. I crouch down sneakily and scurry up behind them before popping up and yelling, "Boo!"

Mom and Dad jump in surprise. Mom yelps. A few of the adults they're talking to laugh. Dad turns around and looks at me with a grin. He's the only person I know who can smile with his whole body. From his mouth to his arms as he pulls me in for a hug, even though I get flour on his shirt.

"And this is our oldest, Airi," he tells everyone. Then he turns back to me. "Testing out your costume?"

"What do you think?" I ask, spreading out my arms.

"Very scary." He looks at Mom, who has gone bright red in the face. "Don't you think so?"

"Airi—" Mom starts.

"I'm not changing, so save your breath," I say.

Mom comes over to me and lowers her voice. She hates "making a scene." That's why I didn't let her see me until now. She'll give in and let me wear my costume instead of scolding me in front of strangers. "Airi, I wanted you to make a good impression. This isn't very respectful."

"What's disrespectful?" I asked. "I'm not being rude. I'm just wearing a costume. I think that's *very* respectful. I put a lot of effort into it."

Mom sighs, and I know I've won. "Aren't you embarrassed?"

"Nope."

Dad puts a hand on my shoulder. "It's fine, Reiko. There's no harm in it."

Mom sighs again. "Let me at least wipe off your face."

I duck her hand and dance away. Dad puts his arm around Mom's shoulders and says, "Let her be *her*." She slips her arm around his waist, and they walk down the driveway toward the rest of the party after Mom stops to pick Kaori up again. He makes her look so short. I hope that I'll be as tall as him one day. I already have his flat nose and too-thick black hair. I like to tell myself that he was just like me as a kid, which Grandma and Grandpa won't confirm.

Down the street, most of the younger kids are heading toward the bouncy castle. The adults are around the grills and the coolers filled with melting ice, talking loudly. Dad gets swept into conversation with an older white man with silver hair. E.J. is already with him—he's too shy to go off on his own—so Dad looks around for me.

"Airi," he calls. I pretend I don't hear him and slip off to check out the table of cupcakes frosted in red, white, and blue. I hate small talk. Not my thing. Mom says that it's polite and it makes people feel comfortable. But I didn't get the polite gene, and all of my small talk gets me scolded.

I look around for the other kids my age. There are a few darting around. Some spot me and stop and stare. For anyone who stares longer than ten seconds—I like to count—I give them a little pageant wave. Tight fingers. Graceful wrist. Smile with no teeth. I learned this when Mom enrolled me in a pageant. She thought it would help me learn manners and etiquette.

Nope.

Bad idea.

I got thrown out after one day. Women who teach pageant classes don't like it when you burp the national anthem. They don't see it as a talent. But it's really hard to hit the right notes so that people can hear the melody. It takes real skill, if you ask me. I practiced it for *weeks*.

The cupcakes are starting to melt in the heat. I stick my finger in a few of them to test their softness. It's the perfect way to check out how good a cupcake is. A too-dense cake that you can't poke through is the worst. Mom won't let me do this test at home when she makes cupcakes for school bake sales. "Nobody wants to taste your dirty finger," she always says. Instead she lets me use a wooden chopstick.

The red-frosted cupcakes are too tough. I can't break through the tops. The white ones, though, split right open. Delicious. Now they have little peekaboo holes thanks to me. I'm about to test the blue ones when a woman rushes over.

"Hey, hey, away from the cupcakes," she says, reaching over to grab my hand. I yank away before she can. "Those are for later. Go get a burger or something."

"You must not recognize a professional when you see one," I say, but she's too distracted by the mosquitoes starting to buzz around the table to listen. There's no way I can keep investigating the cupcakes while she's watching.

I go to the nearest grill. There are a few kids my age getting hamburgers and corn on the cob. I get into line behind a boy with a curly red Afro. He has round glasses like E.J. and so many freckles they seem to take over his face in one big reddish-brown blob. I kind of want to ask him if he dyes his hair, because I've never seen a brown kid with red hair, but I know that if it were me, I wouldn't like that, and it doesn't look dyed anyway.

I feel eyes on me. I get a hamburger and a big scoop of macaroni salad. I cover the hamburger in ketchup and the macaroni salad in mustard. E.J. says that's gross, but it's good. After thinking for a moment, I also draw a mustache on myself with the mustard. It's nice and cool on my face.

I turn to look at the other kids. "Hey," I say. You never know. These kids might be more like me. "Nothing like a burger with ketchup and mustard."

I wait for one of the kids to laugh.

Nothing.

They just stare at me with big eyes.

Then there's a burst of giggles from behind me. I start to smile. But when I look around, I see a bunch of girls smirking at me. They cup their hands over their mouths, lean into each other's ears, and whisper and point at me. One saunters over to the table, takes a piece of corn, and goes back to staring at me. Her group of friends watch. They're sitting on blankets neatly spread out over our neighbor's lawn.

The girl with the corn scrunches her nose at me like she smells something bad. She wears a strawberry-covered headband over her black hair. Mine is longer, but hers is smooth and straight, the way Mom wishes mine were. She's wearing one of those pretty sundresses Mom wants me to wear. It has strawberries on it too. She's even wearing a stick-on strawberry-shaped jewel under her right eye.

"Why are you dressed like that?" she asks. She looks me over with that disappointed look I usually see on adults. So I already know we aren't going to get along. She's one of those kids who thinks she's a grown-up. I know all about those kids. They always want to tell on me or brag about how they're smarter.

"I'm testing out my Halloween costume," I tell her. "What's your excuse?"

"Excuse me?" She frowns like her life depends on it. Her friends follow her lead and frown too. I want to tell her that if she isn't careful, her face will stick like that. That's what people always tell me.

"You're excused," I say instead.

"What's that supposed to mean?"

"Oh," I say. "You said, 'Excuse me.' Like you farted or something."

Her mouth drops open. The girls around her forget to copy her and giggle. I smile. Got them. She puts her corn down and crosses her arms.

"That is *not* what I meant," she says. Her friends cover their smiles.

I make sure to smile even bigger. "Oh, sorry," I say. "I just wanted to be polite. Manners are important." Mom says that a lot.

The girl huffs and goes to sit with her friends. They turn their backs on me.

This isn't unusual. I have trouble talking to packs of girls. And packs of boys too. Packs of other kids my age. Or any age, really. And it's okay. We've never been anywhere long enough for it to matter. There was no point in trying to get along with them when I knew it wouldn't be long before we moved.

Maybe I should have been way nicer, the way Mom is. Smile when someone says something mean and pretend I didn't hear. That's probably what I should do since we're supposedly staying here for good. And that means I might actually have to make friends (according to Dad). Not that I would want friends like these girls.

They start talking like I'm not there. "Who wears their Halloween costume before Halloween?" one says loudly.

"Weirdos," says the girl in the strawberry dress.

"Someone who wants to get ahead of everyone else in candy-collecting," I say. "I've already gotten tons of free sweets."

They burst into more laughter. I don't like their kind of laugh. It sounds mean. It's the kind of laugh where I'm not in on the joke.

I turn away from them and go to sit on the porch steps with my food. Mom sees me and gestures for me to wipe off my face. I make a point to smear more food over my mouth. The burger is overcooked.

I wish we were back at Grandma and Grandpa's.

AFTER ACTION REPORT

Date
Sunday, September 5

Location
Fort Shafter, Hawai'i

Actions Undertaken
Neighborhood
reconnaissance

Welcome barbecue

Duration
Like THREE HOURS (ugh)

Purpose
Learning about our new
neighborhood

Mission Result
Reconnaissance: successful

Barbecue: kinda successful

Remarks
People here don't
understand my sense of
humor yet. They'll need to
get used to me since I'm not
going anywhere. Mom didn't
like my costume much, but
Dad thought it was funny.
Both of them work so hard,
but at least Dad still knows
how to have fun. Mom
just gets more and more
serious every day. Maybe it's
because I'm older and I'm
supposed to get serious too.
But I think I can crack her. I
just have to keep trying.

Reconnaissance is going
good. I've mostly figured
out my way around the
important parts of the base.
I've lived on a lot of bases,
and I know that they're
always easier to navigate
once I've figured out where
things are. They're like their
own little cities. Here, we're
in the middle of Honolulu.
Right next to the airport too
(it's only like ten minutes
away by car). Mom doesn't
like the noise of the planes,
but I think it's cool. I've
been keeping track of the
different logos I've seen.
Here are some.

SITUATION REPORT

Date
Tuesday, September 7

Location
Joe Takata Elementary

Activities Planned
Scoping out my new teacher

Meeting the other kids

Logistical Requirements
None

Obstacles Anticipated
My new teacher

Remarks
I've done this so many times I could do it in my sleep. School here started like two weeks ago, so I won't be as behind as usual, but I still get to miss all the boring first-day-of-the-school-year stuff. Which is perfect.

The only difference between this school and all the others is that we're supposedly staying in Hawai'i for good. So part of my mission today is to figure out who's worth being friends with. Usually there's no point in trying to get to know anyone. And kids don't get me most of the time. They think I'm annoying or weird. Or sometimes they're just racist. And then I don't even want to be friends with them anyway.

The worst part about always being the new kid is that everyone already has their friends. So there's never any room for someone like me. When I was little, sometimes playing pranks with the boys worked. But now we're at the age where boys and girls don't do anything together. Which is silly, because there isn't really a difference, and there are kids who don't even fit those categories anyway. It's just all about how our parents tell us to dress and act. But everyone just ignores me. They don't want to get in trouble.

All of that's just fine with me. If no one wants to have fun with me, then that's their loss. I'll have fun in my own group of one: the troublemaker. Because everything I do is trouble, apparently. Even when it's only a joke like switching salt and sugar, or filling someone's bag with confetti.

Mom would tell me to try behaving for once. But I don't want to make friends because I'm acting like a good kid. Any friends I have should know who I am. So I'm not really expecting much from today. But you never know. Maybe the kids here will be different.

MY NEW SCHOOL LOOKS DIFFERENT FROM THE others I've been to. In the past, it's always been a big chunky building with cement blocks, a black concrete square they call the playground, and a patch of dry grass out front. It's like they want to make sure you know it's one of the worst places on earth.

Instead of one big building, though, this school is a bunch of smaller buildings with covered walkways between them. The walls are painted dark blue, and there's a big grassy field behind a fence that looks perfect for rolling in. The kids are different too, just like on the base. At all my other schools, E.J. and I stood out like blue Popsicles in a box of red. Here there are lots of Asian kids. A lot of them have really tan skin like my cousins. I look like a ghost compared to them.

Mom takes E.J. and me to the office first to get our class

information. I plop down in one of the chairs to wait. This part always takes forever. While we're waiting, one of the grown-ups says they want to talk to her and E.J. about his placement test. Maybe that means he didn't do as good as he thought. Mom looks at me. She obviously doesn't want to let me go alone. She doesn't trust me.

"Can Airi wait here?" she asks the receptionist.

"We can have a student show her to her class." The receptionist gets up and pokes her head outside. She comes back with a kid I recognize—the brown boy with the freckles and red Afro from the barbecue. He's wearing a backpack so full it looks like it's going to burst.

"This is Jason," she says. "He's in Airi's class. Jason, you can show Airi to Mrs. Ashton's room, right?"

Jason looks nervous. He's holding a messy folder in his arms. "Sure."

"Is that okay, Mrs. Sano?" the receptionist asks Mom. "If you want to walk with Airi yourself—"

I picture arriving at my new classroom with my mom. "It's okay," I say, jumping out of the chair. "It'll be great. Bye, Mom!" I wave.

Mom looks like she wants to say something—probably tell me to be good or something—but she'd never do that in front of other people. Not in English, anyway. When we lived in the South she used to speak Japanese when she wanted to scold me in public. She can't do that here. You never know who might understand. Like at the airport on the way here, I said "kutabare"[7] to E.J. because he was annoying me. I must be unlucky, because Mom heard. First she said, "Airi!" but then she said, "In Hawai'i, there will be other people who speak Japanese too." Which means I can't just call people "baka"[8] when they annoy me the way I used to. Then she confiscated my headphones as punishment, so I couldn't listen to music on the plane. And the flight to Hawai'i is *long*.

Instead she says, "Have a good first day."

I salute.

"Um," Jason says when I look at him. "This way."

He starts off down the hall. I follow him. A tall boy sticks out his foot as Jason passes. There's no time to warn him.

---

7   Koo-ta-BAH-reh. I learned this word from the action movies Dad watches. Gangsters like to say it. It means something like "drop dead." Mom got so mad when she heard me say it.

8   BAH-ka, which means "stupid" or "idiot." If you watch anime, you probably know this. It's one of those words that even non-Japanese people like to use (though I think when they say it in their bad accents, it just makes *them* the baka).

He sprawls out and drops his folder. The papers fly every-where. The tall boy and his friends laugh.

Jason doesn't even look to see who did it. He just starts gathering up his work and a few photos. I stare at the tall boy and his friends and memorize their faces. It's always good to know who the bullies are. They're the best to play pranks on. Jason should try. Maybe put superglue on his papers so that if he's tripped, they stick to the bullies like rice. Good luck explaining that to the teachers. Good luck trying to hide that you're a bully.

Jason is taking a long time getting his stuff. He's picking everything up one at a time, which is the slowest way to do it. He obviously hasn't figured out how to speedrun clean-ing. I crouch down and sweep the last papers into my arms.

"Here," I say.

Jason looks at the papers. So maybe they're a little dirty now. Who cares? "Thanks," he says. He takes them back.

"Are they in our class?" I ask.

"No," Jason says. "They're in Mrs. Higa's class. They're jerks."

"Okay." I gesture dramatically, like someone on one of the Asian dramas Mom watches. "Continue."

Jason scrunches up his face in confusion, but he doesn't say anything else. He leads me to our classroom. There are a lot of desks crowded inside. The walls are covered in art. There's a big comfy-looking chair crammed into the corner by the door. It looks a little like how I made my bedroom: stuffed full.

There are two teachers in the room. Which I hate immediately. One teacher is bad enough. Two is twice as much work. It'll take twice as long to teach them who I am. One is young, a little sunburned with shiny light brown hair. She's crouched down next to one of the desks, looking at a kid's homework. The other one is at the front of the classroom, writing on the whiteboard in neat, large letters.

"Mrs. Ashton," Jason says to the teacher at the front. She turns around, already smiling. When she sees me, she smiles bigger.

She has the biggest, curliest, coolest hair I've ever seen. It's like a fluffy storm cloud around her head. There's even a streak of gray that spikes like a lightning bolt. She has brown skin like Jason, but a little darker and without the freckles.

I tug at the end of the French braid Mom pulled my hair into this morning and wish we could change hairstyles. (Mom thinks I look nice with French braids. All I know is that she has to pull so tight that I yell. The long tail is good for hitting E.J. with, though. If I turn my head really fast, I can make it fly. If I time it right, it even looks like an accident.) She's wearing a long skirt with narwhals on it, cat-eye glasses, and a big sparkling ring that looks like a fat, juicy cherry.

"Good morning, Jason," she says. She has a soft voice. Too soft. She's going to be a complete pushover. Not even a challenge. "Thank you for showing our new student to our room." She pats him on the back. He ducks his head while giggles break out through the room and scurries to his desk.

She turns to me next. "You must be Airi," she says. She

actually pronounces it almost completely right. EYE-ree (she doesn't know about the Japanese "r" sound). Not Airy. Not Ari. Once someone even thought I said Alli but with an accent. Mom was really mad about that one. Sometimes I mispronounce their names back to show them how it feels.

"Yep," I say. "That's me."

"I'm Mrs. Ashton. Hattie Ashton, if we're being specific, but you'll be calling me Mrs. Ashton." She winks.

"Hattie like a hat?" I ask.

The class bursts into laughter. Off to a good start. I could get used to that.

"Yes, like a hat. It was my grandmother's name." She points to an empty desk in the second-to-last row, two seats down from Jason. "Why don't you take that seat while everyone introduces themselves, the same as we did on the first day of class?"

Jason I already know. It turns out the girls from the barbecue are here too. Mei is the girl with the strawberry dress. Today she's wearing a dress with pineapples on it. She must really like fruit. Her two friends are named Kiana and Grace. I already know we aren't going to get along. I also recognize a Hawaiian girl named Emma and a Japanese boy named Wyatt from the barbecue, not that I talked to them at all.

It's already way different from every school I've gone to before, because over half the other kids are Asian. From everyone's last names I can tell most are Japanese, but there are a few with Korean, Chinese, or Filipino names. There are only a few white kids, and then there are some Black kids, aside from Jason, and a couple Hawaiian kids. It's kinda nice to look out at a room and not be the only one without peaches-and-cream skin.

They seem to mostly know each other pretty well. One kid, Joey, mentions they moved to Hawai'i last year, but mostly everyone else acts like they all know each other. You can tell from the way they snort or giggle when someone talks, or exchange looks like they're communicating psychically. It makes me feel like I'm looking in through a window at a party that I wasn't invited to.

Class Seating Chart

Joey	Kai	Malia	Olivia	Gavin
Brayden	Sawyer	Sophia	Andy	Natalie
Wyatt	Chloe	Liam	Jasmine	Aidan
Grace	Mei	Whitney	Jake	Emma
Kiana	Airi	Lily	Jason	Zach
Bailey		Ian		Mason

The other teacher is an "educational assistant." Her name is Ms. Nicole. She comes to check on me while Mrs. Ashton greets everyone and goes over some school announcements. When she sees my almost-empty backpack, she frowns.

"Did you not bring any supplies?" she asks.

All my supplies are shoved under my seat in Mom's car. She'll find them later, but today I won't have to do any work.

"Nope," I say. "Guess I forgot."

Mrs. Ashton finishes the announcements and rings a

tiny xylophone with a tiny mallet. Everyone seems to know what this means without being told. They all pull out different things from their backpacks or go to the shelves at the back of the room. Ms. Nicole tells me to stay put and goes to whisper in Mrs. Ashton's ear. I sit still, watching everyone else start writing or reading. I've never been in a class that uses a chime. I've never been in a class where kids could do things without being told. I don't like not knowing what I'm supposed to do. How am I supposed to know what rules to break if no one tells me what the rules are?

Mrs. Ashton comes over to me and squats down next to my desk. "Hey, Airi. Ms. Nicole says you don't have your books with you today. That's perfectly all right. We start every day with independent rotations for twenty-five minutes to warm up into learning. You can read, work on math or a science project, et cetera."

"Why do adults say 'et cetera'?" I ask. "It isn't really a word. Why not just say everything you mean to say?"

"Well," Mrs. Aston says, "it's because—"

"And it isn't said like it's spelled," I say. "I know it's just 'e-t-c.' But it's said 'et cetera.' That doesn't make any sense." I try to keep throwing things at her so I don't have to warm up to anything. School isn't for everyone.

Mrs. Ashton holds her finger up to my mouth. It smells like honey. I'm so surprised that all the things I'd planned to say disappear.

"You're right—it is spelled 'e-t-c.' That's how people shorten it when writing it down. 'Et cetera' is a term from Latin, and it means that similar things are included in the list but not specifically said." She smiles at me. "If you're interested in the origin of words, we can include that in your learning plan."

She lifts her finger. The spell is lifted. I eye her finger suspiciously. I'll have to be on the lookout for that in the future. That trick won't work on me again.

"What if I don't want a plan?"

"We all have plans," she said. "Even me and Ms. Nicole."

"But—"

A blank piece of paper appears on my desk as if by magic, along with the biggest box of markers I've ever seen. They're the fancy kind with two ends, one thick, one thin. I try not to seem impressed. She doesn't need to know that these are the best art supplies I've ever seen.

"What are these for?" I've perfected the art of sounding bored and annoyed. She can't know that I'm excited.

"For today, I want you to tell me about yourself. You can write or draw about the things you're interested in, or what kind of powers you'd have if you were a superhero, or even just what your favorite foods are."

"What would *you* write about?" I challenge.

"Well," Mrs. Ashton says, "I'd tell you that I love tomatoes and papayas, that I have a big garden where I grow avocados, that I have a five-year-old daughter, that I wish I could fly, that my house is haunted—"

"Your house is haunted?" It comes out way too enthusiastic. I quickly try to look bored. "Actually, I don't care. You're probably just making that up. Most people make things up. Someone once told me they'd been abducted by aliens. Complete lies. Nonsense. Utter bollocks."

She laughs. The tiniest little chuckle that sounds sort of like her xylophone. I'm so surprised that my mouth falls open. Teachers never laugh at my jokes. They don't like them or my pranks. Or me.

"You're right. People lie for all sorts of reasons. But I'm not lying about the ghost. She haunts the guest bedroom. Her name is Shari, and she likes my daughter's dolls."

I want to know every single detail about this ghost, but I can't act interested in Mrs. Ashton. Not yet. Not until I figure her out.

"I still don't believe you," I say.

I can't tell if she's irritated, or sad, or frustrated. Her lips don't move. Her eyes stay fixed on mine. She doesn't give it all away like Mom does. I always know the exact moment when I've made Mom mad.

"That's all right," she says. "You don't know me very well yet. You don't know that I'm very truthful."

I shrug. "Okay. If you say so." I pull a purple marker from the box so she'll stop talking to me. She walks away, leaving behind the smell of honey. I watch out of the corner of my eye as she stops to talk to the other students. They all seem happy to talk to her about their independent whatevers.

So she's nice. I've never had a teacher who was so nice before. But that isn't going to save her. Being nice doesn't mean you won't get pranked. But for now I don't have anything else to do, so I might as well write.

AiRi SANO'S FAVORITE THINGS

- ✱ Burping
- ✱ Mr. Knuckles
- ✱ Kaori
- ✱ My bike

- ✱ Pirates
- ✱ Pranks
- ✱ S'mores
- ✱ Halloween

- ✱ Dad's office
- ✱ Annoying E.J.
- ✱ Thunderstorms
- ✱ Grandma and Grandpa's farm

Mrs. Ashton's Sixth-Grade Classroom

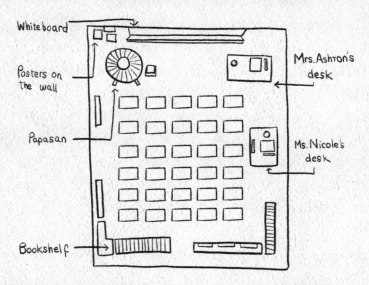

PERSONNEL FILE

Name
Ashton, Hattie (like a hat)

Date of Birth
UNKNOWN

Place of Birth
UNKNOWN

Place of Residence
Oʻahu, Hawaiʻi[9]

Occupation
Sixth-grade teacher

Primary Specialties
Speaking very softly, maybe hypnosis??? (I can't explain her finger trick otherwise.)

Awards and Citations
UNKNOWN

Disciplinary Record
UNKNOWN

Remarks
She's tougher than she looks. She isn't easy to frustrate. But every teacher has their pet peeves. I just need to find hers. I don't like having her pay this much attention to me. I'll have to pay close attention in class to figure her out. I've already started my reconnaissance by mapping out the classroom. Dad says you have to know the terrain.[10]

---

9 I don't know yet if she's a military spouse. That means married to someone in the military. Sometimes old men slip up and say "military wives," but Dad always corrects them because not everyone has a wife.

10 "Terrain" is the area of land you're on and all the details that make it different from other places.

4

SCHOOL CAN'T END FAST ENOUGH. EVEN THOUGH school ends a whole hour earlier here than it did in North Carolina, somehow it feels longer. I don't know if it's because the school is so open and if I just go out the door I'll be able to run far away. Or maybe it's because we moved after the school year already started, so every subject from social studies (yawn) to math (ew) starts with Ms. Nicole handing me a packet of "things to catch up on." I told her that I don't want to catch up on anything. She didn't care.

I used to hate moving during the school year. It always means E.J. and I are behind the other kids. And every school does things differently, so I never know what they're going to be talking about. It's just one more thing that makes me an outsider. So a long time ago I decided not to care. I don't try to figure out what they're teaching us. I've gotten really good at looking like I'm taking notes while I draw instead.

At lunch I stick to myself like I always do. I think about trying to sit with someone else, but all the kids do that thing where they look at you and then look away fast. I know that look. They don't want me to sit with them. Which is fine.

E.J. has the same lunch period as me. He never has any problem finding new friends. I don't get it. He's pretty quiet. And he's a nerd. He likes studying and reading and getting good grades. But every time we change schools, he ends up finding some other kids who want to play his geeky card games with him. It's like having a ready-made friend group. I don't have anything like that. And for some reason people don't react well to me just marching up and trying to sit with them. I gotta figure out my plan of attack if I want to make friends this time. I just don't know where to start.

After lunch we only have forty-five minutes left before we're out. It seems like we should just be able to go home right after eating. I can't wait to get out of here. I'm watching the second hand on the clock spin around. Mrs. Ashton should have a digital clock. This is just kid torture. Dad says there are rules against torture.

We're supposed to be working together with our neighbors to complete a vocabulary sheet from our world history lesson. But I'm sitting next to Mei's friend Kiana, who has no interest in talking to or even looking at me. Probably because of what I said at the barbecue. I heard her telling other people in class about it. I think they want to embarrass me. But joke's on them: I'm not embarrassed. They're the ones who should be embarrassed by having no sense of fun. And I don't care if we turn in a blank worksheet. Zeros are my heroes.

Mrs. Ashton rings her xylophone again. I want to tell her that even though we're still in elementary school, we aren't babies. We don't need chimes to tell us to be quiet or songs to calm us down. She could just tell us to shut up. I know teachers aren't supposed to say that, and neither am I, because when I tell E.J. to shut up, Mom makes me go to my room. But I know about a hundred other ways to tell someone to shut up, and some won't even get you in trouble. She could pick one from my list:

"Shut your traps!"

"Be quiet!"

"Silence!"

"Zip it!"

"You're hurting my ears!"

"Do you have an off button?"

"Noisy, noisy, noisy."

"だまれ!"[11]

"I've had enough!"

"Are you finished?"

And my all-time favorite: "Give me an 'S.' Give me an 'H.' Give me a 'U.' Give me a 'T.' And add an 'UP'!" It's best if you say it like a cheerleader.

But Mrs. Ashton doesn't use any of these phrases. She

---

11 Da-MAH-reh. Be careful saying this around Japanese moms and grandmas, or they might make you weed the garden for hours and hours. It's more polite to say 静かに—shiz-oo-KA-nee—but who has time to be polite?

continues ringing the xylophone until everyone stops talking and focuses on her. They're trained just like soldiers. Everyone snaps to attention.

"Please finish the worksheet at home tonight if you didn't do so," Mrs. Ashton says. "Thank you for working so well together. And now, since we have a little extra time, we're going to read a bit more of our book together."

I groan. Everyone whips around to stare at me like I've just stood on top of my desk and screamed. Mrs. Ashton doesn't seem to notice, but Ms. Nicole frowns at me and holds her finger to her lips. She might be a problem.

"Luckily, Airi, you haven't missed very much," Mrs. Ashton says. She pulls out a large book. "We're reading *The Secret Garden*, and it's just starting to get exciting. Does anyone want to catch Airi up?"

"No thanks," I say before anyone can volunteer.

"All right." Mrs. Ashton hands Ms. Nicole the book and goes to the big comfy chair. She drags it out from the corner.

"Since Airi is new, I'd like to break our reading order and give her a chance to sit in the papasan. Why don't you start today's chapter for us, Airi?"

Mei's hand shoots into the air. She flaps it like she's trying to put out a fire. If it were me, I'd have just shouted out whatever I wanted to say. But she waits for Ms. Nicole to notice and call on her.

"But, Mrs. Ashton, it was my turn to read today," she says. "I was really looking forward to it."

Her friends all nod very seriously. I wonder if Mei is a really good reader or something. They're acting like they've been robbed of a once-in-a-lifetime experience. Mrs. Ashton apologizes and promises that Mei will be next. Ms. Nicole is gesturing for me to stand up. I stay seated.

"I don't think it's fair for me to come in and mess up the order," I say.

Mei actually turns around and smiles at me.

"That's very sweet, Airi, but I'd love to hear you read for us. At least a paragraph or two. Then we can go back to the regular reading order."

"It really isn't fair," I say. I'm starting to sweat. I don't want to have to read. Not out loud. Every time I've done it before I've gotten scolded for not doing it properly, even when I was really trying. I don't know why I should get in trouble for something just because I'm not very good at it. And Mrs. Ashton doesn't need to know my weakness. If I just act difficult enough, she'll let me off. That's always worked before. "Mei wants to read. I don't."

I'm making too much of a scene. Usually I try to stay quiet the first few days of school so I can get the lay of the land before I start to cause trouble. It keeps people in a state of surprise and shock. I have to earn my keep as the difficult kid. That's the only kid I want to be. There are so many different kinds of kids: the quiet kid (I already know that's Jason), the kid who loves math, the teacher's pet (Mei), the one who loves animals, the athletic kid, the one who wants to be a movie star. No one wants to be the difficult kid, except me. The difficult kid gets left alone.

"Just a few sentences, then. I know it's asking a lot of you on your first day." Mrs. Ashton smiles encouragingly. She thinks I'm shy. Which is so wrong. She doesn't know me. She thinks she's going easy on me. I don't want that. I don't want to win because she isn't trying. Or because she feels sorry for me. I don't need her help. I can read a few lines out of a book. How hard can it be? As long as I concentrate really hard I'll be fine—that's what everyone has told me before.

"Fine," I say. I march to the front of the classroom and fling myself into the papasan. It creaks. Ms. Nicole makes a face like she wants to scold me, but teachers never scold on the first day. "Just so you know, I hate reading." That isn't completely true. I like comic books. But that's different.

A few kids laugh.

"I'm sorry to hear that," Mrs. Ashton says. She hands me the book, which has a hard cover and shows a little blonde girl opening a door into a garden. "I hope that in my class you'll learn to love reading."

"Fat chance," I mutter.

"What was that?"

"Nothing."

"We're on chapter five," Mrs. Ashton says. "Right at the bookmark."

Everyone else has their own copy of the book. They're smaller than mine. Why did she give me the big heavy book? It seems very hard to open to where it's been marked. Even my hands are sweating. I look down at the page. The letters seem to swim. I order my eyes to focus. Maybe I need glasses. Even though the doctor says my vision is fine.

"At first . . ." The words are wiggling now. I'm staring at them too hard. I try to press them down with my thumb. I clear my throat and start over. "At first each day . . . which passed . . ." I stop again. I can feel Mrs. Ashton and Ms. Nicole looking at me. I clear my throat again. "I'm really thirsty."

"Just the first few sentences," Mrs. Ashton says. "Tomorrow you can bring a water bottle like everyone else. We have filling stations in the cafeteria. Continue, please?"

I press my finger down so hard that I'm sure I'm denting the paper. "At first each day which passed by for . . . Mary . . . Lennox was ex—ex—" I know this word, I'm sure of it. Or at least parts of it. But the letters aren't arranging themselves into sounds. I hate it when this happens.

"Exactly," Mrs. Ashton says gently.

I hate her now. Even though I can tell she's trying to be nice from how softly she says it. My brain was working, and she knocked me right out of my concentration. I could have gotten it out if she'd just been quiet. "This book is weird and girly."

"I don't know that I agree with that," Mrs. Ashton says. "And what does 'girly' mean, anyway?" She waits a moment for me to answer, but I can't think of anything other than that the book has flowers on the cover. "Please continue."

"EXACTLY," I say, and then I have to look for it on the page again. It takes me too long. The kids start giggling. I grit my teeth. "Exactly like the others," I say as quickly as I can. I put the book down. "I'm tired. Isn't it time to go home?"

"We still have another twenty minutes," Mrs. Ashton says. "But I understand. I'm tired too. Thank you for reading, Airi. You did very well."

Even I know that isn't true. Any other teacher would be scowling at me. Ms. Nicole already is. I've been craving it all day. But Mrs. Ashton just smiles and smiles. So either she was lying about always being truthful or she isn't smart enough to be a teacher.

I get up and go back to my seat. I pass Mei on the way.

"Nice reading," Mei whispers to me. Then she smiles. She's probably been looking for a way to get back at me for what I said about her farting at the barbecue.

"I try my best," I say.

I sit back down. My embarrassment is fading. What does it matter if I messed up the words? Just as long as I don't have to do it again. I don't care that I'm bad at school. But not everyone needs to know about it. Not when they'll think they're better than me because of it.

I put my head down on my arms. It's time to do the one thing I do best at school: sleep. Mrs. Ashton won't interrupt Mei just to wake me up. And I'm right. I doze right until the last bell. Mrs. Ashton says goodbye to me when I leave. I wave cheerily back. Little does she know I'm already thinking about how to get out of reading next time. I have a plan. She'll see.

AFTER ACTION REPORT

Date
Tuesday, September 7

Location
Joe Takata Elementary

Actions Undertaken
First day of school

Duration
8 a.m.—2 p.m.

Purpose
Doing all the new-student stuff: finding the classroom, learning the schedule, meeting the teacher and the other kids

Mission Result
Hard to say. I learned some things about my new school. Mei and her friends don't like me. Mom would say I should have been nicer when we first met. Jason was nice, but he seems like a scaredy-cat. And Mrs. Ashton is a problem.

Remarks
The weirdest thing about this new school is that people don't eat in the cafeteria. Everyone knows the cafeteria tells you who is popular and who isn't. But here they all eat outside, on the grass or on tables. Some sit with their backs up against the classrooms. It's weird. I didn't know what to do, so I ate while walking around and looking at people. But I saw a tree that looks good for tomorrow. I think that might be nice. I wonder what they do when it rains, though, because it rains a lot in Hawai'i. People at my old schools never believed that, but one time I kept track when we were staying with Grandma and Grandpa, and it rained every. Single. Day.

PERSONNEL FILE

Name
Sano, Eric

Date of Birth
August 8

Place of Birth
Honolulu, Hawai'i

Place of Residence
Fort Shafter, Hawai'i.

Occupation
Dad, lieutenant colonel in the US Army (United States Indo-Pacific Command, Eighth Theater Sustainment Command)

Primary Specialties
Cooking chicken (all kinds), finding the ripest avocados, logistics[12]

Awards and Citations
Army Overseas Service Ribbon, Armed Forces Expeditionary Medal, Korea Defense Service Medal, United Nations Medal, Army Good Conduct Medal, National Defense Service Medal

Disciplinary Record
Aunty Jen says that Dad used to catch wild chickens and put them in people's backyards. They are LOUD in the mornings!

Remarks
Dad joined the army because (a) Great-Grandpa was in the all-Japanese unit of the army and got lots of awards, and he and Dad were really close; and (b) he's the oldest of three, and the army helped pay for college.

People always say stuff like "You should be proud of your dad." Which I am, even though I don't have anything to do with it. I know people respect him. They listen when he talks. And I know he works really hard, because he spends a lot of time at work. Sometimes he doesn't come home until way late. And he's usually really tired on the weekends, but he still makes time to take me and E.J. to the park or a movie. Or he used to. He's been working even more lately. I hope that changes here.

---

12 Dad says this means making plans and organizing things. He's really good at that stuff.

DAD IS HOME IN TIME FOR DINNER TODAY. USUALLY he works pretty late. Mom always puts his portion in the fridge for when he comes home. But he's home at five thirty on the dot. He says it's because his new office is so close and he's settling in now. I could get used to that.

Mom has made oyakodon. I like to call it the mother-and-child bowl. That's what "oyako" means. It's because it's made with chicken and eggs. Mom and child. Mom says that it doesn't translate well. We eat it with leftover macaroni salad from the barbecue. Dad adds lots of daikon radish to his plate. I show off by eating my mac salad with chopsticks. E.J. still has to use kids' training

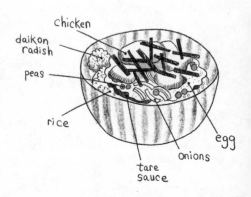

chicken

daikon radish

peas

rice

tare sauce

onions

egg

chopsticks. Kaori smears her food all over her high chair tray.

"How did everyone's day go?" Dad asks. "First day at your new school go all right, guys?" He grins at me.

"It was great!" E.J. says. "Dad, did Mom tell you about my placement test?"

"She mentioned it," Dad says. "What's the news?"

Mom looks at E.J. and says, "You go ahead."

He grins and bounces up and down in his seat. It's the most excited I've ever seen him. "They said that I did so well on my placement test that I could move up a grade if I wanted! I could be in Airi's class!"

"Ugh," I say. Teachers already compare me to E.J. Being in the same class as him would really suck. I slump down in my seat. Just what I need. A know-it-all little brother to draw attention to me. I hope he's just bragging.

"*But*," he says, "they also said that I could get into one of the private schools. They said I could be more challenged that way." He sounds like an adult. I want to give him a noogie.

"They said he might even be able to get a scholarship," Mom says. She looks proud. I've never seen her look that way about me. "Isn't that great?"

"That's amazing, E.J.!" Dad says. "Your mom and I will have to do a little research, but is that something you might be interested in?"

I tune out the rest of their conversation. I'm not interested in listening to them talk about how smart and studious E.J. is. It makes me wanna barf. I focus on Kaori, who is shoving rice into her mouth and getting it all over her face. I see a piece of chicken that didn't get fully shredded and reach over to break it up so she doesn't choke.

"And what about you, Airi?" Dad asks. "How was school?"

I shrug. "It was fine," I say. "E.J. and me share our lunch period. So that sucks."

"Airi," Mom says in a warning voice. E.J. sticks his tongue out at me, lightning-fast so Mom doesn't see.

"Yeah, I never liked it when my sister and I had lunch together," Dad says. "It makes it so much harder to pretend you don't know each other."

"Yep," I say. I focus on my food so that they stop asking me about my day. I don't know how I feel about it yet. Except that it was weird. And different. I haven't figured out Mrs. Ashton yet, and I don't like that. Teachers are like kids. There are different types.

There are the strict teachers who want you to only speak when spoken to.

There are the ones who try to be funny and don't like it when you make jokes too.

There are the ones who try to be your friend so they can trick you into doing work.

There are the teachers who don't like teaching and don't pay very much attention.

Mrs. Ashton seems like the kind who tries to be my friend. But those teachers usually stop trying after I'm rude to them the first few times. She didn't. And she didn't try to act like she understood me. I hate that.

Mom asks Dad how his day went. He started work a week ago, so it wasn't his first day, but he says he's still new. He talks about how much he likes his new commanding officer and his new coworkers. Everyone likes my dad. He doesn't even have to try very hard.

Mom had a good day too. She went to the park with Kaori and met some other moms. Kaori played with some other babies and met a Shiba dog. Mom has pictures on her phone, which I have to admit are very cute. She signed up for a lei-making class for herself and swim lessons for her and Kaori. She sounds excited. I stab at a piece of chicken.

After dinner E.J. stays at the table to do his homework. I go upstairs to my room. I still have the vocabulary worksheet I was supposed to work on with Kiana. It's completely blank. I think it's ridiculous to expect me to do it when I only just got to this school. How am I supposed to know what any of these words mean? I can't even figure out how to say them.

In case Mom checks if I'm doing my homework, I have to hide the evidence. I'll just tell her that I didn't get any because it's my first day. And I bet I won't get in trouble at school since Mrs. Ashton seems to want me to like her. I can probably get away with stuff for a bit before she starts sending me to the office or calling my parents. That's when I have to actually pretend to try, just to keep Mom from scolding me. What I really care about is disappointing Dad. But he doesn't get really upset unless I'm sent home early, and that's only happened once.

So I need to make my homework disappear. I take a pair

of scissors and cut out the vocabulary words. City-state. Mesopotamia. Levees. A lot of the words look cool. I think they'll look good on my collage. I highlight those so they stick out. I'm planning on keeping up the collage all the way until I graduate high school. I figure it's like a scrapbook. A visual history of my amazing school career. (There's no way I'm going to college. I told Mom that once, and she got so upset at me for not "considering my future." I don't see what college has to do with any of the things I want to do with my life.)

Once I'm done with that, I still have a few hours before Mom comes to check that I'm asleep. I go into E.J.'s room and rearrange all the clothes in his dresser. And not in the way you'd expect. I don't just put his socks in his under-wear drawer. I mix them up. Socks, underwear, pajamas, all mixed together. I organize them by color, but not in rainbow order. That's too easy to guess.

After that I go back to my room and start making plans. Mrs. Ashton seems like she's going to be hard to crack. I need to have an attack plan to annoy her into submission. The first step is finding reasons we have to stop reading *The Secret Garden*. I watch some videos on Dad's tablet to see what people say about the book. A lot of them use big words I don't understand, but I memorize them so I can say them back to her. Just saying it was girly wasn't enough. I have to have a real, grown-up reason for why we shouldn't read it anymore. Then she'll listen.

I fall asleep fast. Learning all those words is hard work. But I wake up in the middle of the night because Kaori is crying again. I lie awake in bed and listen to her for a while. But she doesn't stop. That means that Mom and Dad aren't able to get her to sleep. I hate hearing Kaori cry. It makes my chest feel all tight and my eyes sting, like I'm remembering what it's like to be a baby and be unable to do anything ex-cept cry.

I get up and walk down the hall. Mom is pacing around the room with Kaori in her arms, singing to her in Japanese. Usually that will get Kaori to sleep, but not tonight. Maybe Kaori's day wasn't as good as Mom thought. Mom turns toward the door when I step inside.

"She won't go down," she says, sounding exhausted.

"I'm sorry we woke you, Airi. You should go back to sleep."

"It's okay," I say. I hold out my arms for Kaori. "I'll take her."

"No, no," Mom says, shaking her head. "I'll get her to sleep, you have school tomorrow."

Kaori wails louder, and one of her little fists hits Mom in the side of the head. Mom winces.

"You know I can get her to sleep," I say. "Let me."

Finally, Mom passes her over. I let Kaori grab on to the end of my braid as I bounce her up and down. Slowly, she starts to get quieter and quieter. I rub my face against hers, and she giggles. Then she sighs and cuddles into my shoulder. Mom and I wait a few minutes to see if she wakes up again before I try to put her back in her crib.

But the moment I start to put her down, she starts crying. And when we try again a few minutes later, the same thing happens. Finally I go and sit in the big comfy rocking chair with Kaori resting in my arms. "I'll sleep here," I say. "If I hold her all night, maybe she'll sleep."

"Don't be ridiculous," Mom says. "That will be terrible for your back. And what if you drop her?"

"I won't," I say indignantly. But Mom goes and gets the baby sling anyway. Kaori wakes up while we get her into the sling, but settles again easily. I sit back down and close my eyes. Even with my eyes shut, I can feel Mom looking at me.

"You can stay and watch if you're so worried," I tell her.

Mom doesn't say anything at first. "I'll be right back."

When she comes back, I sneak a peek. She's carrying her pillows and a blanket. She settles the pillows on the floor and sits on them so her head is resting against the chair's arm, and drapes the blanket over my legs.

"We'll wait until she's fully asleep," Mom says. "Then you can go back to bed."

Except Mom falls asleep first. She has a very quiet snore. I'm careful not to rock the chair and wake her. Kaori stays fast asleep. Even though I'm tired, I sit there for a long time listening to the AC and Kaori's little breaths. She smells like baby powder and milk.

I don't remember E.J. as a baby. Dad says I liked him right away. We used to run around together. He was my partner in crime. Then E.J. got older and started being all about school. He never wants to play pranks anymore. He tells me I'm annoying.

I hope Kaori doesn't end up like him. I could use a minion. As soon as Kaori can talk and walk for more than three feet without falling over, I'll start training her. No one would ever suspect her. She's so cute. The perfect weapon.

It would be even better if she never grew up at all. If she stayed just like this.

PERSONNEL FILE

Name
Sano, Kaori (kah-OW-ree)

Date of Birth
December 20 (almost a
Christmas baby!)

Place of Birth
Hopkinsville, Kentucky

Place of Residence
Fort Shafter, Hawai'i

Occupation
Cutest baby ever

Primary Specialties
Making a mess, distracting
Mom, being cute

Awards and Citations
Chubbiest Cheeks, Littlest
Nose

Disciplinary Record
Kaori is the best baby in
the world. She's never done
anything wrong. Even when
she used to burp up on my
clothes.

Remarks
I wasn't sure about having
another sibling. E.J. is
enough of a pain. And Mom
was really stressed while
she was pregnant. Dad was
traveling a lot back then. We
were supposed to move to
North Carolina earlier than
we did, but Mom and Dad
didn't want to move while
she was still pregnant, so
we stayed behind while Dad
went ahead. That sucked.
Dad almost didn't make it
back in time for Kaori's birth
because of bad weather.

But then Kaori was born,
and she was PERFECT. I'm
talking cutest baby from the
start. Even when she was
kind of wrinkly and looked
like an old man. The two of
us were best friends right
away. She could happily lie
in my arms for ages. E.J.
still doesn't really know how
to interact with her. He
won't hold her very often
because he's afraid he'll
drop her. So that's one thing
I'm better at than him.

SOMETHING GROWN-UPS ALWAYS ASK ME iS "WHY did you do that, Airi?" Usually with a frown. I always think it's pretty obvious, like when I stuck googly eyes on everything in our refrigerator, or when E.J. and I were arguing all the time over the TV so I put some tape over the remote sensor after I picked a channel.

Before starting this personnel file, I was writing a guide to pranks. For people who don't know where to get started. Or for people who don't understand why they're fun, though they might be lost causes. I've thought long and hard about what makes a good prank, and I thought if I ever met someone like me, I could share it with them. That hasn't happened yet, but I'll include it here. Just for any of you military personnel reading this. Because a lot of you need to have more fun.

MY GUIDE TO PRANKS

Pranks are an art, not a science. Sure, there are ways to plan and optimize[13] your pranks, but really it comes down to feeling. Sometimes you just know an idea is good, and you have to act in the moment. Those aren't always pranks but what Grandma calls "kolohe" (koh-LOH-hay) aka troublemaking. When I have time to plan, though, I follow these rules:

1. The goal is to make people laugh, not to make people cry. So no wrecking things beyond repair or picking on stuff that they're really scared of. For example, I'd never put fake spiders in E.J.'s shoes, because he's so scared of spiders he starts crying when he sees them. Instead, I put them in Mom's purse or Dad's briefcase.

2. It isn't only about you. I do things because they make me laugh, but a lot of times I want my prank targets (or the people around them) to laugh too. Laugh at how cleverly I tricked or surprised them, or at themselves.

3. It's important to be creative, but sometimes the classics (like whoopee cushions!) will do the job just fine.

4. Laughter is the main goal of most pranks, but there are other goals: revenge (usually against E.J.), annoyance (kids I don't like), making a point (like when I put stink juice in the perfume at pageant class), or as an offensive tactic (against teachers).

5. Above all, have fun! If you're stressed out planning a prank, you're doing something wrong.

If you follow these guidelines, I guarantee your life will become two hundred times more fun!

---

13 Dad likes this word. It means "to make things the best they can be."

SITUATION REPORT

Date
Wednesday, September 8

Location
Joe Takata Elementary

Activities Planned
A simple test prank

Logistical Requirements
Water bottle filled with soda

Obstacles Anticipated
Mei seems like she might be a tattletale, so I gotta watch out for her.

Remarks
I have to pick the best moment to unleash my skills. I'm not sure when that will be yet. But it also has to be when I can do it sneakily, so everyone else needs to be busy too. Independent rotations might be the best time.

7

THE NEXT MORNING, EVEN THOUGH I'M SO TIRED I could sleep for a whole day, I get up as soon as my alarm goes off. I have preparations to make.

Dad has an old water bottle from the Air and Space Museum that changes color when you put something cold in it. I fill it with Sprite from the stash of soda in the garage. No one will notice a few cans missing, and I have plans. I hold it up for inspection. It looks just like water. Perfect.

Next I go to the kitchen. Mom is there putting together our lunches. She used to make really fancy bento boxes until I told her to stop. Other kids would always come over and ask why I had food shaped like rabbits. Now she makes us normal food. Today she's making turkey sandwiches.

"Don't forget the mustard on mine," I tell her. There's an

empty coffee cup on the counter, which means Dad has already left for work.

I get milk from the fridge and cereal from the cabinet. I have a special method for eating cereal. I pour the milk into one bowl and the cereal into another. Then I take a spoonful of the cereal and dip it in the milk. E.J. thinks it's ridiculous. I think it's genius. It means your cereal never gets soggy. The best part of any cereal is the crunch.

E.J. comes down later than me, as usual. He sleeps like a log. He never wakes up when Kaori is crying. When Kaori was really little, I was jealous of that. But once she was bigger and Mom and Dad trusted me to hold her, I didn't mind waking up. Holding Kaori reminds me of holding our cat, except that she doesn't scratch me when she wants to be put down.

After breakfast, Mom walks us to our new bus stop, pushing Kaori in a stroller. Kaori is fast asleep. Well, she should be after last night. I wish I could join her. She looks so cozy.

There are some other kids waiting at the stop, including Mei from my class. She's wearing butterflies today. There's a big sparkly butterfly behind her ear and another at the top of her ponytail. She sees me and looks away.

"Okay, we're here," Mom says. She bends down to check on Kaori. Still fast asleep.

"You don't have to stay with us," I tell her. "We aren't babies."

Mom frowns. "It's your first time taking the bus here, though."

I roll my eyes and look at E.J. "You know how to get on a bus, right?" I ask him.

"Duh," he says. He turns his backpack around to his front so he can dig through it. He pulls out a book. I think he's trying to impress the other kids with how smart he is. But I know he's reading a manga.

"See?" I say to Mom. "We don't need you to wait."

Mom opens her mouth to speak, then shakes her head. "Okay," she says. "Be good at school." She tucks some of my hair behind my ear. I shake it back out in front of my eyes when she looks away.

When the bus comes, I line up with everyone else. I've ridden a lot of different buses. Small buses, crowded buses, empty buses, new buses, and old buses. I've ridden so many different types that I've developed my own theory on how to actually make it fun. Or at least not boring.

TIPS FOR RIDING THE BUS

1. Always sit in the back. If you can get the very last seat, that's even better because you can stretch out on it. Sitting in the front means the driver—or the teacher—can see you. They might try to talk to you. That's the worst.

2. Don't touch underneath the seat, unless you're adding to the gum there.

3. You can eat if you're sneaky enough. The trick is to slump down so the driver can't see you in the mirror.

4. Sit in the aisle and put your backpack by the window if you want to sit alone. Most kids aren't brave enough to ask you to scooch. Learn to give them the evil eye to keep people away.

5. Buses will tell you a lot about people. Who sits with who. Who does their homework. Who has a phone and will show off by playing games or playing music. Buses are the best place to do reconnaissance.

When I was little, I used to play a game called Sweet or Sour. It only works if you sit in the back seat, so that's another reason to sit in the back. You look out the rear window and see if the people behind the bus are sweet or sour by waving. Most people wave back. They smile. Those ones are sweet.

But there are some people who won't smile no matter what. They're sour. I like to pull faces at those people. I press my face up to the glass so my nose squishes. I pull my mouth wide with my pinkies and cross my eyes. If I do it enough, they'll change lanes and I can test the person behind them.

Now that I'm older, not as many people wave back. I think it's because I'm not as cute. If I had Kaori with me, I bet I could get everyone to wave. Since I don't, I have to find other ways to entertain myself. My favorite one is Jell-O. You let yourself go limp. Don't move at all. Don't resist. Let the bumps and turns in the road shake you until you're on the ground. It's fun. You never get jiggled the same way.

No one has claimed the back yet when I get on, so I go there and drop my backpack. Mom still hasn't found the

school supplies I hid in her car, so I shoved a pillow in my backpack to make it look full. Which is perfect, because today I need the extra sleep. I stretch out and close my eyes. Time for day two.

After class starts, Mrs. Ashton brings me a few sheets of paper. "I see you still don't have supplies," she says. "You can use the class markers again."

I look at the papers. They have stuff typed on them. So it's not another drawing day. "What's this?"

"Some personality quizzes," Mrs. Ashton says. "I thought it might be a fun way to get to know you."

"I thought that's what yesterday was for," I say. "I wrote you a whole list of things about me."

"And that was very helpful," Mrs. Ashton says. "If it makes you feel better, the other students did this at the beginning of the year too. I'm not singling you out."

I don't know how to feel about that. Instead of replying I look down at the sheets, focusing hard on the letters until they come together into words. "Which Dinosaur Are You?" says one, which seems kinda babyish. Another one asks, "Which Halloween Monster Are You?" That one sounds interesting. Not that I want her to see that.

"This is pointless," I say. "What is a quiz going to tell you about me?"

"Humor me," Mrs. Ashton says.

"Okay," I say. "How do bees style their hair?"

Mrs. Ashton looks confused, so I say it again. She shakes her head and says, "I don't know, how?"

"With a honeycomb!" I say.

To my surprise, Mrs. Ashton laughs her little xylophone laugh. "I like that!" she says. "Maybe you could write down some of your favorite jokes for me if you don't want to do a quiz."

"I can't give away my secrets like that," I tell her. I pull the quiz about Halloween monsters toward me. "I'll do this one."

"Okay," Mrs. Ashton says. "Let me know when you're done, and we can think of something else for you to do."

I decide I'm going to take as long as possible with this quiz. I give her a big smile. "Sounds like fun!"

Yeah right.

WHICH HALLOWEEN MONSTER ARE YOU?

Are you a funky Frankenstein, a vicious vampire, a
wicked witch, a mysterious mummy, or a ghastly ghost?
Take this quiz to find out!

1. What's your favorite subject in school?

   a. History

   b. Art

   c. Science

   d. PE

   e. English

   None of the above!!!! School sucks no matter what.

2. Tell us your favorite color.

   a. Yellow

   b. Black

   c. Green

   d. ~~Blue~~ Teal

   e. Red

3. Which country do you most
want to visit?

   a. Egypt

   b. Ireland

   c. Switzerland

   d. Mexico

   e. Romania ↘

   I don't know where this is. Is it near Rome?

4. Pick your favorite animal.

a. Cat

b. Frog

c. Wolf

d. Owl

e. Bat

5. Lastly, which of the following would you want with you on a deserted island?

a.   Tent

b.   A favorite book

c.   First aid kit

d.   Radio or music player

e.   Sunscreen

How about a boat??

IF YOU ANSWERED MOSTLY A: You're a MYSTERIOUS MUMMY! You have a taste for the finer things in life and like to surround yourself with your favorite things. Your larger-than-life personality sets you apart from your peers. You're either the class clown or the most popular kid in school. Lucky you! But don't let it go to your head.

IF YOU ANSWERED MOSTLY B: You're a WICKED WITCH! You're creative and express yourself best through art. You're more likely to be found watching the crowd than in it, which means people sometimes think the worst of you, even if you don't mean any harm. Try participating in a group activity—you might enjoy it!

IF YOU ANSWERED MOSTLY C: You're a FUNKY FRANKENSTEIN! You may look scary on the outside, but you're really a gentle soul. You love animals of all kinds and are most at home in the outdoors. When making new friends, look for people with backgrounds and interests similar to yours.

IF YOU ANSWERED MOSTLY D: You're a GHASTLY GHOST! Most of the time, you fly under the radar, but you're secretly a bit of a prankster. You like to do the unexpected and take people by surprise, which isn't always appreciated! Be more direct when talking to people; don't make them guess what you want.

IF YOU ANSWERED MOSTLY E: You're a VICIOUS VAMPIRE! When it comes to style, no one has you beat. You don't follow the trends; you set them! Your charm and humor have won you many friends, but be careful you aren't taking more from the people around you than you give back.

It takes me longer than I want to take the quiz, especially when I get to the results. They include so much information that I just kind of glance over them. Mrs. Ashton isn't going to check to be sure I really read the whole thing. All I need to do is count my results: two of my answers mean I'm a witch, two mean I'm a mummy, and one means I'm a ghost.

"Mrs. Ashton," I say when I'm finished. "I didn't get mostly anything. See?" I show her my results. "Your test is broken."

Mrs. Ashton laughs. "You aren't the only one who got a result like that. Looks like you're a mix between a mummy and a witch—why don't you draw for me what that might look like?"

"You're just trying to keep me busy," I complain. "If I'm not going to do real work, you should just let me sleep."

"I can get you some 'real' work if you want," Mrs. Ashton says with a smile. "There's a math worksheet that I assigned last Friday—"

I quickly flip the paper over and start to draw. "No," I say. "This is fine."

Mrs. Ashton laughs again. I shake my hair over my eyes so she can't see me looking at her while I draw. She doesn't seem like she's laughing *at* me, but I don't know. It doesn't make any sense for a teacher to be like her. When I started at my other schools, they'd give me big packets of make-up work or tell me to read the textbook. Then they'd let me do whatever. But Mrs. Ashton is right here. Watching me.

"I'll do this," I tell her. "I still think it's pointless, but if you want me to draw instead of work, I'm not complaining."

"I like to get to know my students," Mrs. Ashton says. "It helps me figure out how best to help you learn."

"Good luck," I say. "No one's ever been able to make me learn before."

Mrs. Ashton grins. "You've never had me as your teacher before." She stands up and taps the edge of my desk. "Work on that for the rest of study time. After this, I promise I'll give you only real work."

I groan loudly and slump in my seat. Mei looks over her shoulder with a scowl and puts her finger to her lips. I cross my eyes at her. I'm really good at crossing my eyes. I spent one whole weekend in front of the bathroom mirror figuring out how to do it. When I showed Mom, she screamed and thought I'd hurt myself. She threatened to take me to see the doctor.

Mrs. Ashton finally goes back to her desk when she sees that I'm working on my mummy-witch. I wait until she's looking down to take out my water bottle. The classroom is really quiet now that we're not talking. It's perfect.

I take a big swig of my Sprite and let the gas bubble up in my chest. It hurts a little when you build up a burp, but the payoff is worth it. You can feel it right between your ribs. I swallow a bit more air—gotta make this one good—and then let it loose.

BRAAAAAAAAAAAAAAAAAAAPPPPPPPPPPPPPPP!

Mei jumps and shrieks. Some of the other kids, mostly the

boys, start laughing. Ms. Nicole, who's helping Mei's friend Grace with something, looks around and says, "Who did that?"

I'm ahead of her. I've already put my head back down over my drawing. I make a little slit in my hair to keep an eye on her and Mrs. Ashton. Mrs. Ashton is checking out the room too, but she doesn't seem mad. Ms. Nicole, though, has stood up and started walking up the aisle. I make sure to look extra focused on giving my mummy-witch a cat that looks like ours, Mr. Knuckles, who still isn't out of pet quarantine.

When Ms. Nicole has made it to the front of the classroom, I sneakily take another sip. It's one thing that's good about my hair—it's so thick that it can hide a lot. It's annoying to have it down, but it comes in handy. I turn my head to the left and let out a smaller burp, cupping my hand around my mouth so that it travels a little. I've learned my tricks.

Ms. Nicole turns around so fast she almost trips. "Okay," she says. "Very funny."

More kids are giggling, though most of them are trying to hide it. That's okay. I can work with this.

When it comes to disruption, it's all about the timing. You don't do everything at once. First of all, that will draw a lot of attention to you. Which is good sometimes, but right now that isn't what I want. Second of all, it's more effective to space it out. Let them think that it's over. Then you get them when their defenses are down.

Ms. Nicole is watching closely. Time to wait. I add a

cauldron with some puffs of steam. A pyramid in the background. I give the witch my hair. But she doesn't have a nose, because mummies don't really have noses. I saw one at a museum once. Mom didn't like looking at it, but I thought it was cool. It would have been cooler if it had come to life like in a movie, though.

Teachers always say I have no patience. But they're wrong. I know how to be patient when it matters. I know how to pick the right moment. So I wait. I wait all the way until Ms. Nicole stops watching us and goes to sit with Mrs. Ashton. Just as she's about to sit—

BRRAAAAP!

Ms. Nicole yelps and falls off her chair.

The entire class bursts into laughter.

Even Mrs. Ashton looks up with a smile.

It's perfect. I got laughter. I got Mrs. Ashton's attention. And I made Ms. Nicole mad. Which I think is fair because she obviously doesn't like me. And no one caught me. Total success.

8

I'M FIGURING OUT HOW LUNCH WORKS HERE. WITHOUT
the clear map of a cafeteria, it's harder to spot the gangs,
but I'm starting to get the hang of it.

There are a few tables, and that's where the older kids
sit. Mei has a table with her friends in a prime spot under
the shade of a banyan tree. E.J. has already found a group of
boys to play his card games with over near the playground.
I've picked out a tree that has nice shade. It's not too near
anyone else, but not too far away. If you sit really far away
from everyone, that's gonna make everyone look at you
funny. And not in a good way.

I sit beneath the tree and take out my lunch. I wish
Mom and Dad would let me have a phone so I could listen to music or play a game when I eat. But Dad says I'm
too young, and Mom says she's afraid I'll break it. I've been

working on some comics, but I hid all my school supplies in Mom's car, so I don't have paper or anything. Should have thought of that. Oh well. I can just watch people today.

Then that kid Jason from my class comes over and sits down a few feet from me. It's weird. No one's ever done that before. I eye him suspiciously. He must want something. That's the only reason I can think of for why he'd want to sit near me. Unless it's just because I helped him with his papers yesterday.

Jason has food from the cafeteria, which doesn't look so bad compared to other schools I've been to. He looks at me, and I look at him. I open my eyes wide so I don't blink first. I don't know what to say. Which never happens.

"I know it was you," he says.

"What was me?" I ask, taking a big bite of my sandwich and chewing with my mouth open. Maybe he'll get grossed out and move away. If we're gonna eat lunch together—which everyone knows is the first step toward a maybe-friendship—he has to prove his worth.

Jason doesn't even flinch. He stares me down. "The burping," he says. "Today in class."

"I don't know what you're talking about," I say. "I didn't hear anything."

Jason raises his eyebrows. He looks like a little old man with his glasses. "Okay," he says. "I just wanted to know how you did it. Burped on command, I mean."

I eye him. "How do I know you don't just want to tell on me?"

He shrugs.

"Hmm," I say. "I thought you were a wuss. You didn't do anything when that boy tripped you yesterday."

"Are you going to trip me?" he asks.

I could say yes. That might get him to leave me alone. But the truth is I've never been like that. The point of my pranks isn't to make myself laugh, even if I usually do. It's to hear other people laugh. And you don't make them laugh by bullying them. That's the first rule in my guide to pranks.

"No," I say.

"Then it's okay." He digs his fork into the perfect mound of rice on his lunch tray and takes a big bite.

I watch him through narrowed eyes. He seems like the kind of kid who would be the teacher's favorite. In class he answers a lot of questions, and he always looks like he's paying attention. I don't know if I should trust him. The thing is, if he were really a teacher suck-up, he'd have told on the kid who tripped him. But he didn't. So maybe he's one of those teacher's favorites who doesn't really try to be the favorite. Those kids are annoying in a different way, but they don't tattle.

"Fine," I say. "I'll tell you." I show him my water bottle.

He looks at it. "Um, okay?"

"Try a sip," I say. Before he can take it, I add, "Waterfall it."

He rolls his eyes and says, "Obviously," before taking the bottle and tipping some Sprite into his mouth. I see the moment he realizes what it is. His eyes go big and round, and he quickly puts the cap back on. "We aren't allowed to have soda!" His voice goes all high-pitched.

"So?" I take the bottle back and give it a little shake. I like to watch the bubbles fizz. "No one can tell."

Jason looks around, like a teacher is going to appear and scold us. When nothing happens, his shoulders drop back down. "That's how you do it," he says. "You get yourself all gassy and just—*brrrp*." His fake burp noise sounds like it came from a mouse.

"It's how you get the really impressive burps," I say. "But I don't need soda to burp." To prove it, I swallow a big lungful of air and let out a *BRRAAAAAP*.

Jason's eyes are wide and impressed. "Wow," he says. "How do you do that?"

I try to teach him, but he can't figure out what I mean when I tell him he has to swallow air. He tries a few times before giving up and eating his lunch. But he doesn't go somewhere else to eat. It's weird. I haven't eaten lunch with anyone like

this in a long time. When I lived in New Jersey, there was a girl named Nadia I used to eat with. She was one of those kids who was really super shy and didn't like to talk to anyone. So I sat with her. Sometimes she'd even ask me about what I was eating. But I moved before we could really get to be friends.

When the lunch bell rings, Jason gets up and goes to throw away his trash. Then he stands by the can and looks at me. I look back, wondering what his deal is.

"Come on," he says. "We're gonna be late."

"You don't have to *wait* for me," I say. "Maybe I want to be late."

Jason rolls his eyes again. "Okay, whatever." He's gotten a little braver. I might have been wrong about him being a wuss. "See you."

I wait until his back is turned to pack up my lunch. I don't want him to think I'm following him.

Back in class, Mrs. Ashton tells everyone we're going to be "working on our projects" today. Everyone seems to know exactly what that means. I'm a little disappointed. I'd memorized all the reasons we shouldn't be reading *The Secret Garden* in case Mrs. Ashton pulled it out again today. But I can wait.

Mrs. Ashton comes to my desk as everyone starts pulling out binders and books. She hands me a packet and says, "Everyone is doing a research project on something from local history or culture. It will include a report on the topic, with your sources cited, a creative piece that can be what-ever you like—there are some suggestions in there—and a poster and presentation that we'll be doing at Parents' Night at the end of the month."

"No thanks," I say, handing the packet back to her.

Mrs. Ashton laughs and crouches down next to me again. I want to ask her if that makes her knees hurt, but that might make her think I'm worried about her. "I know that's a lot of stuff to throw at you all at once," she says. "Why don't we start by having you pick a topic? I've marked the ones that other students have taken."

She sets the packet down on my desk again. I glance over it. There are a lot of words I don't recognize. "What if I don't want to do any of these?" I ask.

"If there's a different topic you'd rather do, we can dis-cuss it together." Mrs. Ashton points at one of the boys in class. "Kai is doing his report on Zippy's."

"The restaurant?" I ask. Dad worked at Zippy's when he was in high school. We still go there when he wants saimin. It seems like a weird topic for a research project.

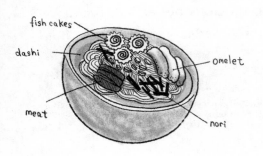

Saimin is a noodle soup made with dashi, fish cakes, and green onions, with Spam or char siu meat, omelet, and nori on top.

"It *is* an aspect of local culture," Mrs. Ashton says with a smile. "Maybe it isn't the first thing someone from the mainland might think of, but if you talked to someone from here, it's something that they know and grew up with."

I look back down at the list. There are so many words. Does she want me to pick one right now?

As if she's reading my mind, Mrs. Ashton says, "You don't have to decide right now. Why don't you look this over and think about it? If you need to talk it over, here's my phone number." She writes it at the top of the page, upside down from where she's looking. I'm impressed but don't show it. "Since you haven't had as much time to prepare as the other students, we can shorten some of the requirements. Let's talk about what you're most comfortable doing tomorrow, okay?"

She doesn't know what power she's just given me. Her phone number? Big mistake. I have to make her think she's safe. So I smile real big and say, "Okay!" before bending over the paper like I'm reading it intently. I hear Mrs. Ashton get up, and I smile to myself. Now I have everything I need to annoy her into leaving me alone.

Local Slang for Haoles

The military is full of haoles (if you don't know what that means, keep reading), so I figure I better explain some stuff to whatever military person is reading this. I'm not an expert, but I know some things. When E.J. and I were little, Mom would take us to Hawai'i for most of the summer because Grandma and Grandpa could help her take care of us. We always visited for Christmas and sometimes Thanksgiving too. And besides, my dad is from here, and he uses these words all the time.

cousin: this isn't just a word for your aunt's or uncle's kid. We also use it for family friends or people in your family who are like cousins but not cousins. Like your parent's cousin. Or really just any family member that there isn't an easy name for.

da kine (duh KY-n): one of the most important words you'll ever learn. It can mean just about anything. It's the same as "whatchamacallit." Like if you can't remember what something is called or just in place of another word.

haole (HOW-lay): Hawaiian word for "foreigner." Usually when people use it, they mean a white person. Some white people get really offended by this, which I think is funny considering how many words white people have for not-white people.

lolo (LOH-loh): Hawaiian word for "crazy." Uncle Dan says this about me a lot, even though calling someone crazy and using that word isn't okay.

the mainland: this is how people in Hawai'i talk about the rest of the US. It's because Hawai'i is a bunch of islands, way apart from the rest. I like saying it because it makes me feel like I'm part of a special group.

pidgin: a big mix of languages: Hawaiian, English, Japanese, Portuguese, Cantonese, Korean, even Spanish! Dad says it's a mixed-up language that was invented on sugarcane plantations in Hawai'i because there were workers from all over (like Dad's great-grandparents from Japan), and they needed to talk to the native Hawaiians and the haoles who owned the land.

9

THE FIRST THING I DO WHEN I GET HOME IS KISS KAORI on the head. Then I go upstairs to "do my homework." That means doing just enough so that if Mom comes to check my work, it looks like I've done it all. Before Kaori was born, she checked more carefully, but now she's too busy, and Dad comes home too late.

Once that's done, I'm bored. E.J. is downstairs actually doing his homework, and if I go down to watch TV, Mom will ask if I've done mine. And if she thinks I'm lying, she'll just look all serious and disappointed. I need something else to do. I've read all my comics—Dad hasn't had time to take me to the store for more—and I don't feel like drawing.

Then I think of the box of tissues Mom keeps next to the bed. That's something I can use. So I go down the hall to my parents' room and carefully pull all the tissues out until there's only a few left. I take the loose tissues over to the closet and start stuffing Dad's fancy shoes with them. I put some in Mom's handbags. I even go to E.J.'s room and fill his pants pockets with tissues. While I'm there, I tie knots in his shoelaces so that when he goes to pull them tight, they'll get stuck.

That's pretty good. I have some other ideas, but they're going to take some more time. One of them I can only do if Mom and Dad let me use the family computer (Mom thinks I'm not old enough to have one of my own, even though E.J. has a game system), and I'll need a reason if I want to convince them. That research project Mrs. Ashton talked about will work. Once I have a topic, I can tell Mom and Dad exactly what I want to use it for. So I'll have to wait.

For now, I take out the packet Mrs. Ashton gave me and flip through it before tearing off one of the pages and folding one edge down to make a triangle. I tear off the extra strip of paper at the bottom and start folding. My older cousin taught me to fold dragons last time we were in Japan. I fold it so the words of the assignment are on the outside, twisting around the wings into the body. I hold it in front of my face and roar as loud as I can.

"Did you say something, Airi?" Mom calls from downstairs.

"Nope!" I yell back.

I put the dragon next to my soup can full of pens. I check the time. It's late enough that I think Mrs. Ashton is probably home. I go back to my parents' room and take their cordless phone back to my bunk bed fort and dial Mrs. Ashton's phone number.

It rings.

And rings.

And rings.

And then Mrs. Ashton's soft voice says, "You've reached Hattie Ashton. Please leave your name and message." Then a little girl's voice shouts, "We love you!"

BEEEEEEEEEEP.

I take a deep breath and say, "HiMrsAshtonIt'sAiri," and start singing the snowman song from *Frozen*. I've been assured that this is the most annoying song to all grown-ups. I get halfway through the second verse when the phone beeps to cut off the message. I hang up and dial again.

Second call: I recite the alphabet backward, then forward, then backward again.

Third call: I sing the opening song from one of the Asian dramas Mom likes to watch, one of the historical ones where everyone wears fancy clothes and is really serious. It's super dramatic. I really belt it out, trying to get my voice to do the wobbly thing that opera singers do.

Fourth call: My voice is getting tired, so I just hum.

Fifth call: The message tells me the mailbox is full and to call back later. "Okay," I say.

Sixth call: Mailbox is full.

Seventh call: It's on the third ring and—

"Hello, Airi," Mrs. Ashton says.

"Who's Airi?" I ask, putting a twang in my voice like the people back in Kentucky.

Mrs. Ashton laughs. "I'm sorry I didn't catch your earlier

calls. I was picking up my daughter from daycare."

That must be the little girl on the voice message. I say, "You should save those messages. They might be valuable one day."

"I wouldn't be surprised," Mrs. Ashton says. "I'm glad you called. Would you like to discuss your research project?"

"I don't know," I say. "I don't think I know enough about Hawai'i to decide." That isn't true. I know a lot about Hawai'i from all the times we used to visit. I could talk about mongooses, or pineapple, or the Japanese-Hawaiian regiment my great-grandfather was in during World War II. I'm just hoping she'll let me do a really easy topic.

"Well, what kind of stories are you interested in?" Mrs. Ashton asks. "I think I remember you said you like pirates?"

"Duh," I say. "Pirates are cool."

"What is it about pirates that you like?"

"They get to do whatever they want," I say. "They don't have to listen to what anyone tells them."

"Do you like the adventure?"

"For sure!" I climb out of my bed and strike a pose like I'm looking at the horizon. "And the battles and the fighting!"

"Hmm." Mrs. Ashton is quiet for a moment. I fill the silence by humming "A Pirate's Life for Me." "I think you might find the story of James Cook interesting. He was a British

captain who was the first European to arrive in Hawai'i."

"Some haole?" I ask. "That doesn't seem like local culture."

Mrs. Ashton bursts into laughter. "Why don't we talk about it more tomorrow?" she says. "I'll find you a summary to read so you can decide if it interests you."

Ugh. Reading. "I'd rather watch a movie," I tell her.

Mrs. Ashton starts to say something but is interrupted by that same little girl's voice calling, "Mommy!"

"Hang on a moment, Airi," Mrs. Ashton tells me. I dangle the phone between my index finger and thumb. Get it? So that it's hanging.

I'm about to just hang up when the little girl talks into the phone again. I bring it back to my ear and say, "Yellow?"

The little girl giggles. "Hi! I'm Eva."

"My name's Airi," I say.

"Is Mommy your teacher?"

"Yeah."

"That's cool." Eva hums a little. "Do you know how to whistle?"

"I do," I say, and I whistle as loud as I can to demonstrate.

"Wow!" Eva sounds so excited. Just from a little whistle. I show off a bit and whistle "Yankee Doodle." "Can you teach me?"

I'm not sure how I'm going to teach her over the phone. But it's better than doing work. "Okay," I say. "You've got to poke out your lips like you're giving someone a kiss."

Eva blows into the phone and giggles. "That didn't work!"

"You have to make your mouth real small," I say. "Squeeze it in. Small as you can."

Eva manages a tiny little toot. "Oh!" she says, surprised.

I spend the next half hour teaching her to whistle until she's got it down. Soon she's whistling "Yankee Doodle" all on her own. Then she starts trying other songs. She's a real whistling whiz, and I tell her so.

"Wow!" Eva says. "That's so cool! Thank you!"

"Oh," I say. "You're welcome." I don't really know what else to say. I've never had anyone thank me like that before. Like they mean it.

In the background, I hear Mrs. Ashton's voice. Eva yells something back.

"Mom says dinner's ready," Eva says. "Will you call again?"

"Maybe," I say. This isn't what I meant to do tonight. But . . . it was okay. "If Mrs. Ashton says it's okay."

"Cool! Okay, bye!" The phone goes silent, and I can't help but laugh. I forgot how funny little kids are. I hope Kaori is like that when she's old enough to talk. That would be fun. I could teach her to whistle too.

I only realize after I put the phone down that Mrs. Ashton didn't really sound annoyed when I called. Even though I'd left so many messages. And then I played with her kid. Over the phone, but still. Not that I would have been mean to Eva just to make Mrs. Ashton mad. I'm a prankster, not a monster.

Mom knocks on my door and pokes her head into the room. "Airi, come down for dinner." She sees the phone in my hand. "Who were you talking to?"

"No one," I say immediately.

Mom eyes me suspiciously. "I hope you weren't making prank calls again," she says.

I've learned my lesson about caller ID. It isn't as fun when the prankee can call back and scold you. "Nope," I tell her. Which is pretty much true, even if my messages to Mrs. Ashton were kind of like prank calls. I don't think it really counts as a prank call if they know who's calling.

Mom doesn't look like she believes me, but she doesn't push. She looks tired. Her eyes have big circles under them. Kaori has been keeping her up too. "Well, put the phone back and come eat," she says. She doesn't close the door when she leaves. I'm always telling her to close the door, even if I'm about to leave. My room is my castle.

I skip down to Mom and Dad's room to put the phone back, whistling the opening to one of the K-pop songs my cousin Layla likes to play in the car. Maybe I didn't succeed in my mission to annoy Mrs. Ashton. But I learned more about her. And knowledge is power.[14]

"You're in a good mood," Dad says when I hop into my seat at the table. Mom flaps her hand at me to try to make me sit properly. "Have a good day at school?"

"I had a pretty good day," I say. "*Despite* school."

Dad laughs. E.J. shakes his head like a disappointed uncle. Mom sighs. Just a normal day in the Sano house.

---

14 Teachers always say this to me. And it's true, but not the way they think it is. Knowing about the farming equipment of ancient Sumerians doesn't help me. If school taught me *useful* things like how to pick a lock or how to stand on my head without getting all dizzy, maybe I'd like it more.

INCIDENT REPORT

Date
Thursday, September 9

Location
Fort Shafter, Mom's car

Event Description
Mom found my school supplies where I had shoved them under the seat in her car. She made me practice my kanji as punishment. I still don't know many characters, but she wants me to be able to write the ones I know *perfectly*. I let her think I hate it, but I actually kind of like kanji. They're like little pictures, and you just have to memorize what they mean and how they sound. You don't have to try to figure anything out. It just means what it means.

THE NEXT DAY BEFORE CLASS STARTS, MRS. ASHTON comes by my desk carrying a stack of comic books that she sets down next to my hand. The one on top has a girl with red hair standing on a pirate ship.

"What's this?" I ask.

"Our conversation last night made me dig up some of the comic books I have at home," she says. "I thought you could use them for your reading log."

"Reading log?"

"Yes." Mrs. Ashton shifts the comic books aside and pulls a sheet of paper out from the bottom. "Everyone has one. You write the name of the book you read, the author, and one sentence about it."

I look at the paper, then at the comics. I don't know why teachers are so obsessed with reading. There are faster and easier ways to be told a story. If Mrs. Ashton makes me focus on the reading part, it'll suck out all the fun. "I'll pass."

Mrs. Ashton laughs. "Unfortunately, everyone has to do it. Even Ms. Nicole and I keep logs that we share with the class."

"How do you know we aren't just making it up?"

"I suppose we don't," Mrs. Ashton says. "We trust you to keep track of yourself."

"That's your first mistake," I tell her. I put my thumb over the pirate girl's face. "You really let people count comics?"

"It's still reading," Mrs. Ashton says. "If you don't want them, you can put them on the class bookshelf in the corner. Take a look, and you can let me know at recess."

"Sure." I wait for Mrs. Ashton to leave.

"Thank you for talking for so long with Eva last night," she says instead. "She took the phone right out of my hands. The two of you seemed to be getting along so well that I didn't want to interrupt."

"It was no big deal," I mutter, kicking the back of Mei's chair.

"Not many children your age would have the patience to teach a five-year-old to whistle," Mrs. Ashton says. "And Eva can be shy."

"Didn't seem shy to me."

"Perhaps because you were talking on the phone instead of face-to-face." Mrs. Ashton smiles at me. "Eva's only been with my wife and me for a year, and it's been a difficult adjustment for her. It's nice to see her opening up to someone."

"Yeah, whatever." I can see a couple of the other kids looking over. I don't want them to think I'm sucking up. Suck-ups are the worst. They spoil the fun for everyone.

Mrs. Ashton finally gets that I'm not up for talking much and says thanks again before going to her desk to do whatever it is she does during our "independent study rotations."

I wait until she goes back to her desk to open the top book. The art in the comics Mrs. Ashton gave me is pretty cool. I expected something kind of old-fashioned, like the ones Dad has in plastic bags. He doesn't let me touch those, but he got an app on his tablet so I could see what they look like.

My last teacher told me comic books didn't count as reading when I brought the *One Piece* manga for silent reading time. But Mrs. Ashton says reading is reading. Which it can't be, because I like comics and I *hate* reading. Art and pictures are way better at telling a story. I've tried explaining this to teachers before, but they've told me to try harder, or that I haven't found the right book. As if it's like finding a pair of shoes that fit. I told my third-grade teacher that reading didn't make sense. He told me to stop making excuses.

For now, I guess I'll think about giving Mrs. Ashton's comic books a try and see how the rest of class goes. I'm sure I'll find some way to show her what kind of kid I am.

WHAT HAPPENS NEXT . . .

THE END

At recess, Mrs. Ashton asks me to stay back. Ms. Nicole is still mad at me for interrupting her history lesson. I'm expecting to be sent to the office, which would be great because I'd be there for a while instead of in class. Or maybe she'll write me up, which would be less great unless I figure out a way to hide it from Mom and Dad.

Instead, Mrs. Ashton asks, "Have you decided what you want to do with those comic books yet?"

I shrug. "I don't know."

"In that case, why don't you take them over to the bookcase?" Mrs. Ashton waits for me to get them from the book basket under my desk before she says, "Since you're already here, would you mind reorganizing the shelf for me? I'm afraid it's gotten a little out of hand, and I haven't had time to put things in order. Looking at the books might give you an idea of what you want to read."

I narrow my eyes. She thinks she's sneaky. But I know a punishment when I hear one. She's watching me with that same pleasant smile. If I say no, she might get mad. Normally, I wouldn't care, but you have to play nice sometimes. Causing too much trouble right away gets your parents called in.

"Okay," I say. I look over to the corner where the bookshelf is. Mrs. Ashton wasn't kidding. The thing really is a mess. If Mom could see how messy it is, she would be so annoyed. Not that she'd say so, at least not to Mrs. Ashton.

I start to pull the books out to check the titles. I've started to pile them in order of the authors' names when I decide that's too boring. Everything's always alphabetical. I have a better idea. And it'll go a lot faster too.

When Mrs. Ashton comes over to check on me, I'm almost done. I step back so she can see what I've done. "There," I say, sliding the last few books onto the shelf. "They're in order."

And they are. Just not alphabetical order.

Instead I've arranged them by color. Which is a better way to sort things. Colors are more interesting and easier to remember. And Mrs. Ashton never said I had to put things in alphabetical order. Just "in order."

Mrs. Ashton puts her hands on her hips as she looks at what I've done. I wait for the frown. The scowl. The frustrated, "Just go, Airi."

But then she laughs. A real, deep laugh, my favorite kind. She looks at me and says, "It's beautiful, Airi."

I stare at her. "It is?"

"It is," Mrs. Ashton says. "You know, organizing by color is very popular right now. You've just made the classroom very chic."

"Chic?"

"It's a French word meaning fashionable and elegant." Mrs. Ashton smiles at me. "Don't you think this little corner looks much brighter now?"

"I guess," I say. I can't believe she likes it. I think Mrs. Ashton might be a little weird. That's gonna make it harder to knock her off-balance. I've already gotten Ms. Nicole to give up on me, but Mrs. Ashton just won't do what I expect. I might need to rethink my strategy for annoying her into giving up on me.

"You've still got a few minutes left of recess if you'd like to go grab a snack," Mrs. Ashton says. "You'll want to have energy for PE."

"I'm not hungry," I tell her, which isn't true. But I don't want her to know that her punishment bothered me at all. She's gotta try harder than that.

"Well, all right. Thank you for helping me out, Airi." Mrs. Ashton smiles.

I grin back at her, showing as many teeth as I can. "No problem." No response, yet again. I need to write these things down. Keep track of her reactions. Until I can find her weak spot.

I may not be making the progress I expected with Mrs. Ashton, but I think I'm getting more settled here. Most of the kids in my class still don't seem to know how to talk to me—I've tried a couple of times, and they haven't been mean or anything, just kind of like "Why are you talking to me?"—but Jason has started sitting near me under my tree every lunch period. Usually he doesn't talk much, and at first I didn't either, because I didn't get why he was there. But he doesn't seem to have anyone else to sit with. So I don't make him leave.

Normally, I'd just say whatever I'm thinking about. But then I remember the barbecue and how Mei and Kiana and Grace all seemed unimpressed by my jokes. Mom's always asking me to think before I speak. But thinking means I never can decide on what to say. It's way easier to just let things come out as they please.

I'm sitting under the tree at lunch on Friday with my notes on my arguments against *The Secret Garden*. It's been a whole week, and I've been practicing, but Mrs. Ashton still hasn't tried to get us to read it again. So I figure I should review.

Grown-ups don't like how I take notes. They say it isn't right. Because when I take notes, I take them so I understand. Which means not a lot of words, and lots of misspellings. Which I don't think matters very much anyway, because notes are just for me, and I don't care if I spelled something wrong.

For things like this, if I have to memorize something, I draw to remind myself of the word. I draw what the word sounds like to me. I'm running over the words when Jason scoots up next to me. I scoot away and frown at him.

"What are you doing?" I ask.

"What are *you* doing?" he says back to me. "Are you actually studying? You haven't even turned your homework in all week."

He must have noticed because we sit near each other. Every morning when Ms. Nicole comes around to collect homework, I give her a new reason why I don't have it. Today I said my cat ate it. Which would be impressive since Mr. Knuckles is still in pet quarantine. Ms. Nicole frowned and told me that Mrs. Ashton is going easy on me this week (which normally I wouldn't mind, but the faster I get her to stop that, the less time we'll waste pretending to like each other) and that I'd better have my homework done next week.

"I'm rehearsing," I tell Jason.

"Are you in a play or something?"

"A movie," I tell him. "It's about ninjas. My cousin is a movie director." That's kind of true. Cousin Caroline is a film student. She did do a short movie about ninjas. It was super cool.

"Yeah right." Jason looks at the index card I've written on. "What's that supposed to be?"

He points at the drawing I have in the middle. A sneaky-looking little boy with devil horns and a tail.

"It's an imp," I tell him.

"What's an imp?"

"Like a tiny devil. Or a demon." I make a scary face at him. "They're troublemakers. I can relate."

Jason laughs. "Okay." He scoots away and picks up his plastic cup of pineapple. "What's it really for?"

"You'll see," I tell him. Jason looks interested. I'm starting to think maybe he has potential to be a partner in crime. Which makes sense. The quiet kids always want to have more fun. They just don't know how. I'll have to consider teaching him—if he can be trusted. I'll have to figure out a way to test him.

My preparations pay off, because that afternoon Mrs.

Ashton finally pulls out the papasan chair and announces we're going to read from *The Secret Garden* again. She's about to call up the next person in order when I raise my hand.

"Airi!" Mrs. Ashton smiles. "Would you like to read?"

"No," I say. "I don't think we should be reading this book at all."

"Is that so?" Mrs. Ashton sets the book down on the chair. "I welcome everyone to bring up any concerns they have about the material we cover in class. Why shouldn't we read this?"

Now is my chance. I've practiced my argument so I get all the words right. I've memorized it exactly the way I heard it on YouTube. "It's a cultural relic that romanticizes British imperialism and racist attitudes toward Indian people, and the plot being about a girl performing domestic duties like homemaking and gardening promotes sexist stereotypes. It's outdated and irrelevant."

The classroom goes very quiet. Mrs. Ashton purses her lips. *This is it*, I think. *I've finally made her mad.* Now she'll send me out of the classroom and I can sit in the hall while they read. If I sneak out a pencil with me, I can doodle on the wall. That's what I used to do when Mom put me in time-out. I feel like I've conquered a mountain. Finally. Let's get it over with. The first time the teacher gets mad is always the worst. And the longer it takes, the worse it is.

But then Mrs. Ashton laughs.

Laughs.

I scowl and slump in my seat. She isn't even taking me seriously. Not that I thought she would. But I didn't think she'd laugh at me over it. And not like she thinks I'm funny. Like she thinks I'm ridiculous. That's the worst kind of laughter. The kind that makes me want to shrivel up in a ball.

"Now, I must say that isn't what I expected to hear," Mrs. Ashton says. "That was a very mature and thorough answer, Airi."

My head jerks up. I stare at her. She's looking at me, still smiling, but she seems serious. I've never been called mature before. Usually the opposite. I'm *proud* of being immature. "What?"

"Those are all valid and important criticisms of *The Secret Garden*," Mrs. Ashton says. "Class, I'm sorry to do this, but we'll have to do a make-up reading session next week. Right now, I think it's important to address Airi's concerns."

"But, Mrs. Ashton—!" Kiana says. It was her turn to read. She probably wanted to show off how good she is.

"I promise we'll catch up, Kiana." Mrs. Ashton goes to the board and writes the word IMPERIALISM. It doesn't look anything like how I thought it would be spelled. "Let's add this to your vocabulary," she says. "It's a big word, and a big concept. Does anyone have any idea what it means?"

One of the boys raises his hand. "Don't they say some-thing like that in Star Wars?" he asks when Mrs. Ashton nods at him.

Mrs. Ashton laughs and nods. "Yes, that's right. 'Imperial' refers to an empire. You're probably thinking of the Imperial stormtroopers. In this case, Airi is talking about the British Empire, which during Mary Lennox's time was so large that it was said the sun never set on it." Below that she writes *EMPIRE*. "We've talked a bit about empires in social studies. Can anyone define it for me?"

Mei raises her hand and says, "It's a big kingdom."

"That's a good way to think of it," Mrs. Ashton says. "But it's a little more than that. An empire is a group of countries or people that is ruled by one person. In *The Secret Garden*, that was Queen Victoria. The British invaded and conquered a large number of lands, including India, where Mary grew up. Airi's criticism is important, because the British Empire treated the people they ruled unkindly. In this case, Airi's use of 'imperialism' refers to an empire's policy of forcing their culture, religion, customs, and interests onto another group. Can anyone think of another example of this?"

"The Roman Empire," suggests one girl.

"Good," Mrs. Ashton says. "Anyone else?"

Emma raises her hand timidly. When Mrs. Ashton calls on her, she says in a voice so small it could be from a mouse, "Maybe America taking over Hawai'i?"

Mrs. Ashton actually claps, looking pleased. I roll my eyes. "Excellent, Emma! Yes, the United States' annexation of Hawai'i was an act of imperialism. You'll learn more about this next year in social studies, but a group of mostly American businessmen worked to overthrow Queen Lili'uokalani and established their own government, leading Hawai'i to eventually become a territory of the United States.

"The reason it's important to talk about this is because imperialism hurts many people. Airi, you weren't here yet when we read the opening of the book, but we talked a little about Mary's racism toward her Indian caretakers and how that behavior is inappropriate. I'm glad you brought this up, because we should acknowledge that this book was written by someone with a positive view of the British Empire. If any of you think you see a place in the book where this opinion shows up, you should mark it down, and we can discuss it when we finish the book."

"Isn't it bad to read it, then?" I ask. I don't raise my hand. "If the book is bad, why do you like it so much?"

Mrs. Ashton nods. "A good question, Airi. I like this book because it tells the story of a lonely little girl who makes a place of her own where she can express herself. When I was young, I found it very inspirational. I even tried to make my own garden, but it turns out I don't have much of a green thumb." She smiles. "It's good to bring a critical eye to everything, even things you like. Thank you for reminding us of that, Airi."

I groan and slump down farther. This isn't how it was supposed to go at all. Mrs. Ashton was supposed to get embarrassed and say we'll stop reading it. "What about the gender stereotypes?"[15] I ask.

"Those are also worth thinking about," Mrs. Ashton says. "But first let's discuss why we associate gardening with girls."

I groan even louder. So much for that idea.

---

15 This was one of the terms I learned from YouTube. I had to look it up. It means what people expect from boys and girls. Like that all girls like pink and flowers and princesses, and that all boys like fighting and sports and big trucks.

AFTER ACTION REPORT

Date
Friday, September 10

Location
Joe Takata Elementary

Actions Undertaken
First test prank

Called Mrs. Ashton a bunch

Presented reasons we shouldn't read our class book

Duration
One week

Purpose
Figuring out how my class reacts to pranks and finding any tattletales (none yet)

Annoying Mrs. Ashton enough so she stops wanting to help me or teach me or get to know me

Getting class reading time canceled

Mission Result
Test prank: successful

Everything else: failure

Remarks
After I complained that all of the information was hard to read, Mrs. Ashton gave me a list of videos I could watch on YouTube that counted as research for my project on James Cook. If it had been Mr. Simmons (the social studies teacher I had in New Jersey), he'd have told me that's part of the project. If it had been Miss Robertson (my fifth-grade teacher in Kentucky, before we moved to North Carolina), she'd have said that I'm not going to get any special treatment. I can't tell what Mrs. Ashton's deal is. She doesn't act like a teacher. It's weird. I need to think more about this.

As for my classmates, they seem to be getting used to me. Mei and her two best friends still don't seem to like me, but Emma Kapono takes the same bus from base and has started saying hi.

I've been making observations about other kids in my class. The newest kid moved to base early last year. Dad says most people who live at Fort Shafter have pretty settled jobs. They aren't deployed as often because they work at the "Pineapple Pentagon" (that's what Dad's office is called).

Dad's job is the reason we move around a lot. He's some kind of logistics genius. That's what I've heard his coworkers say before. So he gets assigned places to get them organized. Most of the military kids' parents here have permanent posts on the base, so they don't have to move so much. It's weird, because we're all army kids, but they have it way different.

It must be nice to have stayed with the same people in your class for so many years. You get to know everyone better. I've had to get really good at figuring everyone out. Here's what I know so far:

- Mei, Kiana, and Grace: the kind of popular, smart girls who usually have no time for me. It probably isn't worth trying to be friends with them.

- Wyatt and Liam: Best friends who do everything together. They're great at skateboarding. That's what they spend all lunch doing.

- Emma: Nice but quiet. She's a music kid. She spends a lot of her lunches practicing violin in the music room.

- Jason: I think he wants to be friends. That's the only thing that explains why he keeps sitting with me. I think I might like being friends with him. He's funnier than I thought. And a little weird. He seemed more like E.J. But maybe I just thought that because he has glasses. I should know better than that. Maybe making friends won't be as hard as I thought.

11

FRiDAY NiGHT MEANS NO HOMEWORK. IT MEANS I can put my latest idea into action. This one has nothing to do with Mrs. Ashton. It's just for me. I spend a while looking for good photos of garden gnomes. I keep a tab about James Cook open so when Mom comes to check on me it looks like I'm doing research. But really I'm making posters advertising a missing gnome.

I use our home phone number on the posters. I thought about putting Mrs. Ashton's down, or Dad's cell phone, or my cousin Noah's house, but it isn't any fun when I don't get to see what happens at the end of my pranks. I hope people actually call, even though I know they probably won't. I have my answers all planned out.

If they ask me what he looks like, I'll say, "He has big, beautiful eyes."

If they tell me they think they saw him, I'll say, "I'm so glad you found him. We've been so worried!"

If they say they found him, I'll say, "Will you let me talk to him so I know he's okay?"

Or maybe I'll yell and cry, "We won't pay ransom!"

I heard that last one in an action movie Dad was watching with E.J. Dad says ransom is the money you pay to kidnappers so everyone comes home safe. Mom got really mad when she heard us talking about it. She even started scolding Dad in Japanese for letting us watch something "too mature" for our age.

I print out some copies while Mom is feeding Kaori and tell her I'm going for a bike ride. Mom looks nervous, but I promise to stay on the base and come back quick. I won't need too long. Just enough time to tape up my signs.

Not that I put up all of them. That would be a waste. Some I save for school. Some I save for the next time I go with Mom to the mall or the grocery store. There's no rush. It's not that kind of prank. It's just to make things a bit more fun. For everyone.

I have to hide the flyers under my shirt when I get home, because Dad is pulling into the garage just as I'm riding up. He gets out of the car and waits until I wheel my bike in to shut the door.

"Hey there, Airi." He pulls me into a hug. I groan dramatically but hug him back. Dad gives the best hugs. "Did you have a nice ride?"

"Yep."

"You're getting taller." Dad makes a show of measuring me against his chest. "We might need to get you a new bike soon."

"I like my bike," I say. "If we get a new one, I'll have to decorate it up to my standards."

Dad gives a big, deep laugh as he opens the door to the house. Mom's making curry, Dad's favorite. He breathes in deeply and pats me on the back. "Go see if your mom needs help in the kitchen while I get changed."

I go into the kitchen and wash my hands before going to look into the pot. Mom only put about half the curry blocks in, so it's still a little watery. "Did you put carrots in?" I ask. I don't like carrots that much, but for some reason they're really good in curry.

"Yes, I did," Mom says. "Could you get the chicken out of the refrigerator and the panko from the cabinet?"

That means Dad is going to make chicken katsu to go with the curry. I get out an egg too—it helps the panko stick, according to Dad—and flour. Mom sees what I'm doing and gives me an approving nod. When Dad comes downstairs, changed into shorts and an aloha shirt (he's got a ridiculously large collection of them), I've set everything out just as Dad taught me.

Separate plates for the flour and panko. Egg, beaten, in a little bowl.

"Look at this mise en place,"[16] Dad says. "So professional! Thank you, Airi." He ruffles my hair. "Tell your brother to come and wash the rice."

E.J. is the best at washing rice, except for Mom. Dad and I get too impatient. But they will keep rinsing until the water runs perfectly clear. We have a fancy rice maker that Mom bought in Japan. It can do almost anything. You can even make big fluffy pancakes in it. We only do that on the weekend though.

Curry is important business. You need a lot of stuff to make it just right.

First there are the curry blocks. The best brand is the one that uses apple in the recipe. It doesn't taste like apple, it's just a little sweeter. But it makes a big difference.

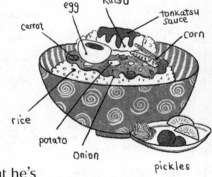

Next there are the ingredients. I like potatoes. E.J. likes corn. Dad isn't picky, but he's always excited when Mom puts in a yam. Mom tries to sneak green beans in there sometimes, but she's started putting them on the side for herself since the rest

---

16 Pronounced meez-on-PLAHHHS. Mom's friend in Tokyo (she's a chef) taught us that. It's French. It means having everything you need for cooking set up and ready.

of us don't like them. The carrots and the potato and onion have to go in early so they get nice and soft. Corn goes in to-ward the end.

Then there are toppings. Usually we do pork or chicken katsu. At restaurants you can get shrimp on it too, but Dad says it's too much work. Mom also likes to put hard-boiled egg on hers. When E.J. was little, he used to eat his curry only if he had a hamburger patty with it. Dad says that means E.J. is a real local boy, because it's kind of like loco moco. Sometimes we put tonkatsu sauce on too.

Last are the pickles. You wouldn't think it, but Japanese people *love* pickles. Not pickles like the ones we have in the US (although there *are* pickled cucumbers). They're called 漬物 (tsukemono, pronounced tskeh-MOH-no[17]), and there are lots of different kinds. There are little onions (らっきょう aka rakkyo, prounounced rah-KYO) and different kinds of radish (my favorite is たくあん aka takuan, pro-nounced ta-KOO-ahng) and eggplant and gobo and even little plums. The pink ginger restaurants give you with sushi is pickled too.

There's a special kind of mixed pickle that goes with curry, called 福神漬 (fukujinzuke, pronounced foo-koo-JIN-zoo-keh). It's hard to find except in Japanese grocery stores, so Mom has always made it herself. Dad says hers is better than store-bought. The recipe isn't always exactly the

---

17 You have to say the "t" and the "u" like they're almost not there. Just the ghost of a letter. It touches your tongue and that's it.

same, because some ingredients are harder to get than others. But there's always eggplant and cucumber and radish, and it all gets mixed up with soy sauce and sugar and vinegar. It's so good. I always put a big scoop on my curry.

When I get my plate, I like to mix everything together. E.J. always makes a face at this. He likes to keep all his food separate. If we have chicken and rice, they can't touch. When he eats curry, he puts everything in neat layers. When he takes a bite, it's like a cake. He says that's how you get a perfect bite. I say that he can't criticize how I eat cereal if that's how he's going to eat curry.

We all eat dinner together around the table, even Kaori. She mostly rubs curry on her face, but she eats some potato too. After dinner we argue over what movie to watch. Dad and I win: *Star Wars*. The original. E.J. falls asleep halfway through. Mom puts Kaori to bed while Obi-Wan is fighting Darth Vader. Then it's just me and Dad, saying the dialogue along with the characters.

I lean into Dad's side as Luke pilots his X-wing toward the reactor core. "Use the Force, Luke," we say at the same time. Dad squeezes my shoulders. It's perfect.

Kaori screams all night. I don't think she likes our new house. I think it's too hot for her, even with the air conditioning on. Or maybe it's the hum of mosquitoes that you can hear even through the windows. Or it could be all the weird new smells: fresh paint, new carpet, and floor polish instead of Dad's cologne and Mom's dashi broth.

I know Mom and Dad are happy with the new assignment. Dad likes being home, and I heard Mom telling Grandma that the weather reminds her of Innoshima Island in the summer. It's kind of funny, because I used to complain about visiting Hawai'i. But that was mostly because the flight is so long and a lot of times we'd be helping Grandma and Grandpa around the house, so it wasn't really like a vacation. But now that we live here, we have all the good stuff and all the normal living stuff without feeling annoyed about how it's supposed to be a fun holiday with nothing to do.

I slip out of bed and down the hall to the nursery. I crawl on all fours, like Kaori would, and peek through the open door. Mom is holding Kaori, who is wiggling and screaming. Snot runs from her nose to her mouth. Fat, angry tears stream down her plump red cheeks. Her eyes are clamped so tight you can hardly see them.

Mom rocks Kaori back and forth, humming. Then she starts to tell her a story.

"Once there was a little girl who never liked to sleep, like you. She would lie awake and pick her teeth with a little wooden toothpick. When she finished, she would put it under her bed instead of throwing them away like she should."

I think that sounds perfectly reasonable, but I want to hear the rest of the story. I flop down to listen.

"Then one night when she was lying awake, the little girl heard a strange noise. It sounded like warriors fighting! It was so close and so loud that she was very afraid. She finally worked up enough courage to look, and do you know what she saw?"

Kaori wails louder. Mom sighs and kisses her head. She looks tired. I wonder if I ever listened to Mom's stories when I was a baby. I don't listen to her much now, if I'm honest. And I probably should. When I was little, and she was upset because I'd done one of the million things she hated, she would try to talk to me and get me to explain why I'd done it. Now she mostly gets quiet. Like she doesn't want to talk to me.

Kaori isn't getting any quieter. That's how I know it's my turn to step in. I'm the Kaori Whisperer. I'm like that man on TV who can get dogs to behave, except that I can get babies—especially Kaori—to settle down.

I stand up and sneak up behind Mom. Kaori is waving her little hands around. I catch one and let her grab on to my finger. Kaori opens her eyes in surprise. When she sees me, she stops crying.

"Airi?" Mom turns as much as she can while not pulling Kaori away from me. "What are you doing up? You scared me."

I coo at Kaori, who reaches out for me. Mom lets me take her. She sniffs at me as she passes Kaori over. "Did you shower? You still smell like kitchen oil."

"Bathing is overrated," I say. "Did you know that ancient people almost never bathed?"

"Well, we aren't ancient people," Mom says. "Please shower."

"Okay," I say. Kaori burrows into my neck, getting snot all over me. She doesn't seem to mind how I smell. I need to warm up to new bathrooms. I'm not used to this one yet. I bounce Kaori a little. She hums.

"I'm serious, Airi," Mom says. "You want to make a good impression, don't you?"

Instead of answering that, I ask, "What happens next in that story?"

Mom looks surprised. "You were listening?"

I rock Kaori back and forth. "You said she heard fighting. What did the little girl see?"

Mom looks like she wants to lecture me more, but instead she sits in the little rocking chair next to Kaori's crib. "She saw a whole army's worth of tiny warriors. Fighting, dancing, singing, playing games. They were making such a racket the girl was afraid they'd wake her parents.

"The little girl was sure she was dreaming, but even though she pinched herself very hard, she didn't wake up. The tiny warriors were still there, still making so much noise that even though she was very sleepy, she couldn't fall asleep until morning, when the little warriors had finally left."

Kaori is starting to settle down in my arms. I hum to her like Mom was doing earlier. She's starting to get hair finally. For a long time she was almost completely bald. I liked that because we could have her wear funny hats. But I like her hair too. It's so soft, like feathers.

"The little girl was afraid to tell her parents what had happened. She was sure they wouldn't believe her. So she didn't tell them for days and days, and every night the tiny warriors came back and made even more noise than the night before. Soon the little girl was so tired that she was falling asleep into her rice, and she couldn't pay attention to any of her studies. Her mother was very worried and kept asking what was wrong.

"Finally, the little girl told her mother about the tiny warriors. Her mother wasn't sure if she believed her daughter, but she said she would sleep in her daughter's room that night and see for herself. Sure enough, she was woken by the tiny warriors. She looked very closely at them and saw that they carried little pieces of wood instead of swords. When at last the warriors left, she picked up a piece of the wood they had left behind and recognized it as one of her daughter's toothpicks.

"She showed it to the little girl the next day and explained that for a tiny warrior, wooden toothpicks were the perfect size for swords. They would, of course, prefer needles or pins if they could have them, but people don't leave needles lying around on the floor. The mother then asked why there were so many toothpicks under the girl's bed.

"The girl was very embarrassed and admitted to her bad habit. Her mother told her to sweep up all the toothpicks, even the ones between the cracks of the wood, and to stop throwing her toothpicks on the floor. The little girl did as she was told, and sure enough, that night the tiny warriors didn't come. And they never came again, because the little girl became very diligent at sweeping her floor, and whenever she used a toothpick, she was sure to throw it away."

Kaori is asleep in my arms, so I whisper when I say, "If I were her, I'd have rallied the tiny soldiers into an army for myself. Maybe she could have set a trap for them."

Mom purses her lips, the way she does when she's trying not to smile. I don't see that look often, but it's almost as good as when she laughs. "Airi, that isn't the point of the story."

"I think tiny warriors sound like a lot of fun," I say. I bend my head to whisper in Kaori's ear. "Don't you think you'd want some tiny warriors?"

Mom stands. "You should go to bed too. I don't want you to tire yourself out."

I don't really want to let Kaori go—I like feeling her tiny breaths against my face—but I am getting pretty tired. I settle Kaori into her crib like Dad taught me. I slip the arm of her plush octopus into the hand holding my finger so she doesn't know I'm gone. I make sure she has her blanket and is in the right position to sleep through the night. No tiny warriors will wake her up.

"You're good with her," Mom says. She tries to hug me around the shoulders, but I slip away to check on the fan. Kaori doesn't like it hot in her room. Mom says it again, like she thinks I didn't hear her. I did. I just don't know what she expects me to say. I know I'm good with Kaori. That's all I seem to be good for.

Mom sighs. "Make sure you get some sleep, okay, Airi?" She yawns. Her yawns are very quiet and elegant. Dad and I yawn loudly, so everyone can hear. "If Kaori wakes up again, your dad and I will take care of it, okay?"

"Sure," I say, but we both know that if Kaori doesn't stop crying, I'm the only one who can make her stop. I may not be good at school, or following the rules, or speaking Japanese, or being polite or quiet, or even being nice, but I am good with the baby. That much I know. And Mom knows it too.

"Good night, Airi," she says. I salute her and lean down to kiss Kaori's cheek. Then I march off to bed like one of the soldiers I saw out earlier this week. I take a peek back to see if Mom is smiling, but her back is to me. So I shut myself in my room. Maybe I'll make myself some toothpick warriors for under my bed.

12

IT'S THE SECOND WEEK OF MY NEW SCHOOL. BY NOW I'm sure Mrs. Ashton is going to push me to do more work. But when she sees me sitting with an empty desk during our independent rotations, she doesn't come over to scold me. Instead, she asks me to write a paragraph on my favorite food. She's been doing weird stuff like this. Sometimes she wants me to play word games. She called Monday's task a "creative exercise." On Tuesday she asked me to write down some words she said. She's weird.

Everyone in class seems excited on Wednesday. They're all whispering to each other and grinning and giggling. I don't know why. It doesn't seem like a special day. It's just a normal Wednesday. I ask Jason about it during recess, and he says that it's because there's a sub in PE. Which I guess is cool. It's always fun to have a sub. They let you get away with a lot more, and when there's a sub for PE it's like having a second recess.

I follow everyone else out to the blacktop. The substitute teacher tells us to do whatever, but that we'd better be moving around. "No sitting," she says. Then she pulls out her phone.

Mei and a bunch of the other kids are whispering together. They wave Jason over, and he goes. I didn't think he was friends with them. They all look back at me. That's never a good sign. I cross my arms and look away.

But then Jason calls me over too. I shuffle toward him. Mei is wearing a kiwi outfit today. Her hair is pulled back into a tight braid instead of loose. She looks very serious.

"Jason says we can trust you," Mei says. "Just so you know, if you tell on us, no one will ever talk to you again."

She's so dramatic. It isn't like they've been talking to me anyway. "Oh no," I say. "What a tragedy."

Mei rolls her eyes. "Whatever. Okay, we have a game we can only play when there's a sub. It's called Extreme Tag."

"Okay," I say. "Have fun."

"Don't be stupid," Mei says. "We're inviting you to play."

My stomach gets all fluttery. I can't remember the last time I got invited to join something. I try not to look pleased. I don't want Mei to think I'm desperate for friends.

"We aren't allowed to play it anymore ever since Wyatt broke his arm last year," Jason explains. "And it isn't called Extreme Tag. It's Murder Tag."

Now that, I like the sound of. "That's a better name."

Mei rolls her eyes again. I think again about telling her that her face will stick that way. That's what Grandma tells me when I make a face. "Of course it is, but we can't call it that, because if any of the teachers hear us talking about Murder Tag, we'll all get in trouble."

"How did Wyatt break his arm?" I ask. You have to know all the dangers of a situation before going in. That's what Dad says.

"He fell off the slide." Mei shakes her head. "He was doing so well too."

Even though I don't want to be interested, they've got me wondering. "Okay, so what's this dangerous, forbidden game?" I ask.

The rules turn out to be pretty simple. Just like any game of tag, there's a person who's It, and they have to catch the others. There are the other rules, or the ROE—Rules of Engagement—as Mei calls them, which are things like "no tag-backs" and "no grabbing of hair or clothes" to keep it fair. All of which are pretty normal. The difference is *how* you catch the others.

The playground is made up of a bunch of connected platforms. There are monkey bars and two slides and a fake rock-climbing wall, plus a wobbly bridge and a spiral pole you can slide down. The platforms are dark brown. That's where the special rule comes in.

The person playing It is the only person allowed to touch the ground. Anyone else who touches the ground becomes It. There's a safe path between the two slides so you can make a big loop around the structure, but that's all. That seems simple enough. It's kind of like Lava Monster. The real twist is what It is allowed to do. They can climb on the play structure as much as they want—they just can't touch anything that's dark brown, like the platforms. If they do, they have to drop back down to the ground and count to five.

It sounds thrilling. It sounds dangerous. I'm in.

Mei starts as It. Apparently the whole game was her idea to begin with. I'd have never guessed. She seems too prissy to play games like tag. But she's vicious. She climbs like a monkey on the outside of the structure, shimmying up the railings. She gets her friend Kiana in the first two minutes of the game. Then it's on.

Wyatt is the only one who doesn't play. He's the referee, because he doesn't want to break his arm again, and he has the loudest whistle in the class. He keeps a sharp eye on if It is touching the platform, or if someone puts a foot on the ground. When he sees anyone doing something they shouldn't be doing, he whistles and yells out their name. So everyone's sure to follow the rules.

I get tagged by Emma, who chases me all the way up the slide. I'm trying to jump down to the safe zone to run for the other side of the play structure when she scrambles up a pole and tags my ankle.

"Airi's It!" she yells, and Wyatt repeats her so everyone knows.

I drop to the ground and take in my surroundings. No one's running just yet. They want to see where I go. Smart.

There's a clump of kids on the other slide. Emma has scrambled up and over where I was and is peeking around the corner through the railing. Jason is standing at the monkey bars, ready to go. It's a risk to do the monkey bars, because if you time it wrong, someone can get you by the legs. Mei is sitting on top of the spiral bit.

Then I spot my target. The one person who hasn't made it up to safety. It's Liam. He's just starting up the ladder. But I can catch him before he gets to the top.

I start running. Liam doesn't see me coming. Everyone else is scattering. I grab the sides of the ladder—the steps are brown, so I can't use those—and swing my feet up to brace below my hands. I can't do this for long, but I can do it for long enough. Have you ever been in a hallway that's narrow enough for you to press your back against one wall and your feet against the other? And you can kind of climb up that way? That's what it's like.

I scramble up. I reach out. I catch his ankle. Liam turns, his face like the 😦 emoji. I smile at him.

"You're It," I say.

I get the rest of the way up while Liam is dropping to the ground. I have a little time to breathe because of the no tag-backs rule. I quickstep down the stairs to where Jason is now about to jump on the rail. It's a long track that connects

two parts of the structure, and you hold on to the grip and send yourself zooming down to the other end. You have to get the right amount of momentum or you won't make it far enough. And if you're too tall, you have to be careful not to let your feet touch the ground. If you're really good, you can get to the other end and then immediately fling the grip back to the first end so anyone on that platform with you can't get away. Or send it going so fast that the person on the other side can't grab it fast enough. I'm really good at that. I got Mei's fingers earlier.[18]

Jason and I look at each other. This is how early friendships die.

"Sorry," Jason says, and he jumps on.

I run away, back up the stairs, and drop to the opposite side of the platform from the ladder, where the rock-climbing wall is. If I hold on to the rock-climbing chain, I can get enough swing to clamber onto the side of the slide.

Wyatt yells, "Malia's It!"

I try to get up. But my hand is slipping. Grace peeks out from under the roof of the slide. If I'm not careful, she could knock me off. I get my leg over the side. Then I thump onto the slide, just as Grace starts to slide.

She hits my back, and we go flying down the slide. We're both yelling. I go shooting off the end, skidding across the rubber protective padding. It's supposed to help cushion

---

18 The handle went zipping toward her too fast and she missed when she tried to grab it. So it pinched her fingers against the end of the rail. I know from experience that hurts a lot.

your falls, but it's made of little bits that crumble and scrape. My left hand and knee catch my fall. From the burning sting, I can tell without looking that I scraped them. Then Grace comes tumbling into me, and I get pushed farther.

"Crap," I say.

"Omigod." Grace peeks down at me. "Airi! Are you okay?"

I roll over with my legs kicked out. My knee and my palm are bleeding. My knee is worse. It actually looks kind of cool. I poke at it. It feels like pushing at a loose tooth. Like, it hurts, but it's not so bad.

"Ew, don't do that!" Grace says. She gets up and waves frantically at Wyatt. "Time-out!"

Suddenly everyone is standing around me and talking. Mei pushes her way to the front and holds out her hand to help me up. Then she says, "Someone take Airi to the nurse's office while I distract Ms. Yamashita."

"I'll do it." Jason raises his hand and pushes his glasses up. "Do you need help walking?"

I scoff. "From this?" I wiggle my leg. Some blood runs down to my sock. "This is nothing."

It does hurt, though. It's starting to feel all weird and cold. Jason doesn't complain that I'm walking slowly. Meanwhile, Mei is talking to the substitute and pointing toward the playground. I bet she's putting on a good show. She seems like the kind of kid who can cry on command. I never figured out how to do that.

I wait until Jason and I get into the hall and around the corner, out of sight, before I poke him hard in the shoulder. "This is your fault," I tell him. "If you hadn't taken the rail, I wouldn't have run that way." I'm only joking, but Jason actually looks guilty, his eyes going big.

"I know," he says. "I'm sorry."

"Don't be sorry—it's everyone for themselves." I look at Jason from the corner of my eye. "I didn't think you'd be so ruthless. I like it."

He blushes. It makes his freckles almost blend into his skin. "Oh."

"Hey, how come you have red hair?" I ask. I feel like we're friendly enough now that he'll know I don't mean it in a rude way. "Does your mom let you dye it?"

Jason reaches up and pulls at one of his curls. "No. This is just my hair. My grandma has red hair too."

"That's cool," I say. "My hair is boring. It's just really thick. I want to dye it something cool, like purple."

"You don't think it's weird?"

"Sure it is," I say. "But weird isn't bad."

Jason scuffs his foot along the floor. "I guess."

I want to say something to cheer him up. But I'm no good at that kind of thing unless I'm pulling a prank or making a joke. I don't think he'd like a joke right now. I think I'm a little nervous. Jason could be a friend. I don't want to mess it up.

The school nurse is a white woman with short-short

hair. She tsks when she sees my leg and makes me sit on the little cot even though I'm not tired. "What happened?" she asks as she takes out the antibacterial stuff. I bite the inside of my mouth to distract myself from the sting.

Over her shoulder, I can see Jason's eyes widening. Does he think I'm going to tell on them because I got hurt? As if. "I tripped," I say with a shrug. "My shoelace wasn't tied good."

"Well, try to be more careful," the nurse says. She gets a really big Band-Aid for my knee and wraps my hand in gauze. It looks like I got in a fight. Mom is going to freak out when she sees it. "There you go. You should be okay to go back to class."

When we get back to the playground, everyone looks at me all worried. But there's no teacher with me, and I give Ms. Yamashita a big smile and say, "I'm okay," before going to stand with Wyatt.

"I'll help you referee," I say. "I won't be able to escape as well with this." I hold up my hand. Everyone makes suitably impressed noises.

I don't tell anyone what I said to the nurse, but Jason must have, because after PE ends and we're going back to Mrs. Ashton's, Mei skips up next to me.

"Thanks for not telling," she says.

"Duh," I say. "It's a fun game. Did you really come up with it?"

Mei tugs at the end of her ponytail and grins smugly. "Yeah."

"That's really cool," I say sincerely.

Mei's mouth opens slightly in surprise. She stares at me for a moment, then smiles again. "Thank you." She twirls her hair around her finger. "Sorry I was kind of mean to you before. You're okay."

"You're okay too," I say. "So far."

Mei rolls her eyes. "Whatever," she says, and she skips on ahead to join Grace and Kiana. But she doesn't seem annoyed or mad. Maybe we could be friends too. I never thought I'd want that. But it seems kind of nice. Having a bunch of friends, I mean. It's like having a team.

AFTER ACTION REPORT

Date
Wednesday, September 15

Location
Joe Takata Elementary

Actions Undertaken
Extreme Tag aka Murder Tag

Duration
One class period

Purpose
Playing a game without the teachers finding out we were playing

Winning

Mission Result
I didn't win, but I was only It once, and the teachers didn't find out, so I think it was successful.

Remarks
Extreme Tag is super fun. I'm surprised the whole class played—it's hard to get that many kids to all agree on something—but it makes sense. I know that I'd want to play if I saw other kids playing it. My knee has gotten a pretty good scab, but the one on my hand is getting in the way when I try to draw. So I'm watching the videos Mrs. Ashton recommended for my research project. Some of them are pretty boring, but there are a couple that are funny. I can't believe she's letting me use videos for a research project. I'd say she's a pushover, but I know she isn't. She's too smart for that, so that must mean she has a different reason.

SATURDAY IS ONE OF MOM'S BAD DAYS. THAT'S WHAT Dad calls them. On Bad Days, she mostly stays in their room. She used to have them every once in a while, but since Kaori was born, she's had them more. It's a little like she's sick but without a fever. She gets all tired and sad and has a hard time doing much.

I used to try to cheer Mom up on her Bad Days. I tried all kinds of things. Singing to her, making her favorite food, talking to her. But Mom always just wants quiet. Or to be alone. It's frustrating because it doesn't *look* like anything's wrong with her. No sneezing or coughing. But she isn't herself. She doesn't even scold me, she's so tired. That's when you know something is wrong.

Dad packs us up, even Kaori, so Mom can rest. That means I get to sit up front because the back seat of Dad's car is too crowded with Kaori's carrier. It would be better if Mom didn't insist I use a booster seat. I try to convince Dad that I don't need one—I'm eleven, not a baby—but he insists. I wish I were taller. Then I wouldn't have to use it.

We drive over to the other side of the island to Grandma and Grandpa's farm. The road is called the Likelike Highway, which isn't pronounced the way you probably think. It's said like LEE-kay LEE-kay. It's a Hawaiian name. I still don't get everything about the pronunciation of Hawaiian words, but I like that there aren't extra letters that don't mean anything. Every letter in a word makes a sound.

I love Grandma and Grandpa's farm. It isn't like the kind of farm you're probably picturing with a big red barn and cows. The main thing they grow is Christmas trees, which have these thick, almost rubbery needles. There are also soybeans and mangoes and a few chickens. Also wild chickens, but Grandma always has my cousin Noah chase them away because they make too much noise in the morning.

The farm is big, and it's pretty near a beach. If you stand in the right spot, you can see the ocean over the top of the neighbors' houses. There are mountains close too. They're covered in trees that are so pretty and green. That's because the farm is on the windward side of the island. Even though rain is annoying (and it rains there all the time), I like it when the clouds come in, because it makes the mountains look so mysterious. I want to climb them all.

My cousin Noah also lives on the farm with his mom and dad and little sister, Aria, who's four.[19] They have their own house that has air conditioning, which is why we usually hang out there when we visit. Grandma and Grandpa always say they don't need it, because the air through the jalousies[20] is good enough. I wish they'd change to normal windows, because I always have to clean them when we visit, and it takes so long.

Noah's mom is my dad's little sister, Aunty Laura. They have another sister, Aunty Jen, who lives in San Francisco. Dad is the only boy. Most of our other cousins are older and don't want to hang out with us. That's okay, though, because

---

19 Aunty Laura's husband, Mike, is white, so our family says Noah and Aria are hapa-haole. I've asked Dad about it before because hapa really means half-Hawaiian, which we aren't. Dad's family is *from* Hawai'i, they aren't *Hawaiian*. There's a big difference. Dad says it's complicated, but we've both started saying half-white instead.

20 They're like shutters except that they're in the part of the window where the glass would usually be. You can turn them so that there's more air coming in, but they still keep the rain out. It kind of sounds like the word "jealousy." Dad says that's because it's the French version of the word. I don't know why you'd be jealous of a window.

Noah and I have lots of fun. One of our favorite things to do is go exploring in the Christmas trees. People like to throw junk over the fence because the trees hide everything. We've found lots of interesting stuff.

THINGS NOAH AND I HAVE FOUND IN THE TREES

- ✭ Lots of trash (yuck)
- ✭ A bunch of DVD cases but with no DVDs inside
- ✭ A bag full of stuffed bears that Aunty Laura said were called Beanie Babies. Apparently people used to collect them because they thought they'd be valuable one day.
- ✭ An entire refrigerator

- ✭ Most of a car with all the electronic parts torn out that we turned into a fort using some blankets until Aunty Laura found out and made us stop because it was "dangerous"
- ✭ A super-old computer with a see-through outside and a big curved screen
- ✭ A bicycle that Grandpa fixed up so Noah could ride it
- ✭ A plastic jewelry box full of costume jewelry
- ✭ A broken vacuum cleaner

Today, though, I need Noah to teach me to catch geckos.

"I was thinking of asking you to catch them for me and putting them in a jar until Monday, but they might die," I say to him, when we leave the grown-ups to hug and talk story. "And I need them to be alive. So I'm gonna need to catch them myself."

"What's on Monday?" Noah asks.

I tell him my plan. He grins wide and says, "That's awesome! I wish I could be there."

This is why Noah is my favorite cousin.

We spend most of the morning in the yard and back in the trees. Noah's super fast when he sees a gecko. His hand snaps out like a blur. He says it's because his mom always screams when she sees them in the house.

"One time we were at Grandma and Grandpa's," I tell him, "and a gecko came out from behind their picture of Jesus on the wall over the sofa. Mom was vacuuming the carpet, so she just lifted up the end and sucked it right up."

"Whoa!" Noah's eyes go wide. "That's so cool."

I thought it was too. I tried to tell Mom that, but I don't know if she got it. I even drew her a picture of her vacuuming up the gecko and stuck it in the book she was reading.

Aunty Laura went to pick up lunch, so we have galbi and rice and noodles, but she made her own mac salad, because hers is the best. Noah and I fight over the Hawaiian Sun, but I get the lilikoi lychee and he gets stuck with guava, because I'm the guest.

Us kids eat lunch sitting at the little low folding table

that they always pull out when we have big family parties. I sit cross-legged and hold Kaori in my lap. The adults eat at the kitchen table so Grandma and Grandpa can be comfortable. Dad checks on us a few times, but I know I have to cut things up for Kaori. I make her a plate with squares of tofu and the noodles cut into baby bites. She isn't a picky eater.

Dad and the other grown-ups are talking about adult stuff, job things and taxes or whatever. It's boring, so I don't listen until I hear Aunty Laura ask, "So you're staying for real? You won't be reassigned again?"

I focus on Kaori so they can't tell that I'm listening. Reassignment is bad. It means we're moving again. And there are some things I like about moving, like getting to see new places, but it also means Dad is gone a lot more because he has to go ahead of us.

"I've asked for this to be my permanent post," Dad says. "I don't like having to move around so much, not with three kids."

Aunty Laura tsks. "Then you shouldn't have joined the army."

Aunty Laura doesn't like the army. She and Dad argue about it sometimes, though they never really get mad at each other. Grandma says arguing is how Aunty Laura and Dad show that they love each other. Aunty Laura thinks Dad could have done a lot of other things instead of being a soldier. Dad likes that it's our family's legacy.

"You sound like Reiko," Dad says.

"I knew I liked her," Aunty Laura says.

"Your twenty years will be up soon," Grandpa says. "Are you going to stay on or retire to be a farmer like me?" Grandpa was a technician at the military base. He fixed machines. He still fixes stuff for the neighbors all the time.

"I haven't decided," Dad says. "It depends on Reiko."

I frown at the top of Kaori's head. I've never heard Dad say anything like that before. I thought he would never want to leave his job. The thought of it scares me. Because what would he do? Wouldn't that mean things would completely change for us? And what does he mean about Mom? Maybe she wants to move back to Japan? I know she misses home. Once she even said she thought I could benefit from going to school in Japan. I think that sounds terrible. She says that in high school you even have to go to class on Saturdays!

Kaori starts whining and wiggling out of my arms. I quickly set her down on the carpet and watch as she walks over to Dad. I love watching her walk. It's more of a waddle, like she's a little penguin. She holds her hands out like she's on a tightrope.

Dad scoops her up and pats her butt. Everyone coos over Kaori. As they should. She's the cutest baby in the world. I look down so they don't know I was eavesdropping. I don't know if I want to hear any more. My plate is pretty much empty, so I say to Noah, "Wanna go outside again?"

"Take your plate to the sink," Dad reminds me.

I salute and march to the sink holding my plate in front of me. "Hup, hup," I say, putting it down. "Hup, hup," I say, marching to the door.

"Get out of here, silly girl," Grandma says, flapping her hand at me. I salute her too.

Noah and I chase the chickens around until his dad comes out to take him to karate class. I go back inside and poke around Noah's room. His room is pretty tidy. Tidier than mine. So I move things around a bit. I tie his shoelaces together and put a textbook under his pillow. I heard once that if you sleep with a textbook under your pillow, you can absorb the information. It's never worked for me, though. I can't wait for him to find all the things I've done. He'll definitely call the house to complain at me. But then he'll laugh. I think he'll like the textbook-under-the-pillow idea. Maybe he'll be able to absorb it.

I get down on my hands and knees to crawl to the living room. I wanna sneak up behind my dad and scare him. Or try to. He's hard to startle. I press myself up against the corner of the hallway. It's a stealth mission.

But then I hear Dad's voice. He's talking quietly, the way he and Mom do when they don't want us to overhear.

"—she isn't adjusting as well as we'd hoped," Dad is saying. I stop and hold my breath so I'm as quiet as I can be. "We thought maybe being here with family might be good for her. But it seems like she's still struggling."

"You've only been here a little while," Grandma says. "Give it time."

I back up a bit. Are they talking about me? I haven't told Dad anything bad. As far as he knows, I love it here. And I do. I like being in Hawai'i. It's true that I've gotten used to moving a lot. I don't have to bother learning about anyone. It doesn't matter if I get in trouble at school. But I'd rather be in Hawai'i than anywhere else. We're near Grandma and Grandpa. The food here is way better than anywhere else we've lived. We can go to the beach every weekend if we want. It doesn't snow (although I will miss snowball fights with E.J. and Dad). And I even have my own room now. It's really a big improvement.

Even school has been okay, which I never thought I'd say. Sure, Mrs. Ashton is weird. Honestly, I'm still waiting for her to blow up at me. I just want to get it over with already. But Jason is an almost-friend. Even Mei has been friendlier since the game of tag. I've even started planning how to become actual friends with them. I've never bothered doing that before. So Dad's wrong. I'm adjusting fine.

I get to my feet and stomp a bit so they hear me coming. I put on a big smile. They won't see me struggling.

"Airi!" Dad is sitting on the couch with Grandma. She's knitting something bright green. "Are you ready to go pick up Mr. Knuckles?"

Mr. Knuckles! I almost forgot! His two-week quarantine is up. That means we can bring him home. "You bet," I say. "Let's go rescue our missing friend."

Dad laughs. He doesn't look at me like he's worried. "Okay," he says. "Go get your brother, and we'll go."

I salute again. "Hup, hup," I say.

PERSONNEL FILE

Name
Mr. Knuckles

Date of Birth
Unknown, but we celebrate it on New Year's Day

Place of Birth
Fayetteville, North Carolina

Place of Residence
Fort Shafter, Hawai'i

Occupation
Cat

Primary Specialties
Purring, snuggling, catching mosquitoes

Awards and Citations
Stinkiest Poop, Prettiest Eyes (a perfect shade of yellow-green)

Disciplinary Record
Got put in time-out in the bathroom when he dragged a dead skunk into the house in North Carolina

Remarks
For a long time we didn't get a pet because we were moving all the time. We were supposed to stay in North Carolina for a few years, which was why Mom and Dad let me and E.J. pick out a cat from the shelter. We picked a grown-up cat because Mom said she didn't want two babies in the house at the same time. The name the shelter gave him was Tortilla. They named all their shelter animals after food.

When Dad applied for the placement in Hawai'i, I thought we were going to have to leave Mr. Knuckles behind. I was ready to throw a tantrum even if I'm "too old" for that—I had my argument points planned, even—but E.J. was actually the one who started crying and said we couldn't leave him behind. So Mr. Knuckles came with us. He REALLY did not like the plane trip. I'm so happy to have him back now.

SITUATION REPORT

Date
Monday, September 20

Location
Joe Takata Elementary

Activities Planned
Making friends using the following strategy:

1. Sit with other people at lunch (I have a head start on this because I've been eating with Jason)
2. Let them in on some of my pranks
3. Share snacks

First targets: Jason Hamilton and Mei Ishida

Logistical Requirements
Snacks (I know where Mom keeps the Pocky, and she never checks the strawberry flavor because she doesn't like it, but I need some others too.)

Obstacles Anticipated
Mei already has two really good friends: Grace and Kiana. I don't see them outside of school, so there isn't really a good chance to get to know them. But Mei takes the same bus as me. Which means she lives near me. Lots of people have school friends and home friends. Home friends are people they'll hang out with at home but will only wave at during school. I think that would be okay. I don't have to be the most popular kid in school. Even if Mei only wants to hang out on the base, that would be a success.

Remarks
Sharing snacks was how I met my first and only best friend, Becky Albright. This was in Virginia, when I was in second grade. I had Yan Yan, and she wanted to know what it was. After that we always split our different desserts. Her mom made really good rugelach that she would bring.

Becky was really into horses. She wanted to be a knight. We went horseback riding once, and it was really fun but also kind of scary. Horses are way bigger than they look. And mine didn't pay any attention to me. It just did whatever it wanted.

Becky actually moved first. Her dad got reassigned to New York. We did video calls on our parents' phones for a while, but they were hard to schedule. Then we moved too, and our time zone changed. Her family still sends us holiday cards, though. Becky has gotten really good at horseback riding.

ON MONDAY, I SIT NEXT TO MEI ON THE BUS TO school. At first she doesn't say anything to me, even when I Jell-O all the way to the floor. When I pop back up and start to do it again, she looks at me with a scowl and asks, "What are you doing?"

So I explain the rules of Jell-O to her, which means I can check step two off my list. She sniffs and says it's immature. I shrug. "What's the point of being a kid if you don't get to be immature?" I ask.

Then I relax my whole body and let the bus shake me back to the floor.

This time when I pop up, Mei has put her backpack to the side. Looking at me suspiciously, she copies me. Or tries to. She just bounces.

"You're too stiff," I tell her. "You have to go completely limp. Like you're going to take a nap."

She gets jiggled a little way off our seat before she catches herself on the seat in front of us. I'm already half-way off our seat. "Let everything go," I say very seriously. "Feel the flow of the bus." At my school in Virginia, we had a PE teacher who was really into yoga and meditation. The teacher would lead us through breathing exercises and say things like "Imagine you're made of dandelion puffs," and "Let all the tension flow from your body." Usually I just fell asleep.

"You sound stupid," she tells me, but she still drops her arms. The bus goes over a big bump, and she gets popped like popcorn. She shrieks as she slides to the floor. Then she starts laughing.

"See?" I'm almost all the way under the seat in front of us. "It's fun."

We get some of the other kids on the bus to play too. E.J. won't because he thinks he's too good for everything I do, but the really little kids like it a lot. We make too much noise, though, because the bus driver yells at us to be quiet. I put my finger to my lips and shush the little kids. Then I slither back down to the floor.

Once we get to school, Mei says, "Bye," and skips off to join Kiana and Grace. Which I expected. That's okay. It's still early.

At lunch, I go to find Jason, but he isn't in the spot he usually is. Instead he's by one of the flower beds near the offices.

He has a big plastic box on a cord around his neck. A butterfly comes by and lands on top of one of the flowers. He
unfolds the plastic box and brings it to his face. He presses
a button, and there's a loud *CLICK* and a flash of light. The
butterfly flaps away.

"What's *that*?" I ask.

Jason jumps and turns. His plastic box is spitting out a
piece of paper. "What? This?" He takes the piece of paper,
which is a white square with a black square in the middle,
and puts it facedown on his leg. "This is a camera."

"I've never seen a camera like that before," I say.

"It's super old," Jason said. "From, like,
the eighties. It's called a Polaroid."

"Like in that one song?"
He doesn't know what I
mean, even when I sing a bit
of it. "Aren't you supposed to
shake it?"

"No!" Jason covers it with
his hands like he thinks I'm
going to grab it and start waving it around. "That messes up
the colors."

"Can I see it?"

"It needs some time to develop," Jason says. "I'll show
you when it's done."

Today, I have a ham sandwich and a container of mango
from Grandma and Grandpa's farm. Jason has two Spam
musubi wrapped in plastic. He carefully unwraps them and

eats them in small bites. When I eat musubi, I always put as much of it in my mouth as I can.

"Are you an army kid too?" Jason asks through a mouthful of rice.

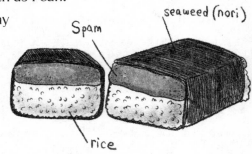

"Yep."

"Where did you move from?"

"North Carolina," I say. When he asks, I list off the places we've lived: Arkansas, Kentucky, North Carolina, Texas, Virginia, New Jersey, South Korea. I was actually born in Japan when Dad was stationed there for a bit, but I don't remember anything about it. Jason whistles, impressed.

"That's a lot of places," he says. "How long are you staying here?"

"I don't know," I say. "It's supposed to be a while. Maybe forever. What about you?"

"We've been here since I was six," he says. "We used to live in California."

"That's cool. My Aunty Jen lives in California." I hold out my container of mango. "Do you want some?" Mom always brings food as gifts for people. When she was still working, she always baked for her coworkers. Now she bakes for my and E.J.'s teachers. It always seems to make people like her. So I figure if I do the same thing, it'll help people like me. It's only a theory. I haven't tried it since Becky. It hurt a lot when she moved away. It's better—and way easier—not to worry about making friends. But Jason is nice. And we're sticking around this time. So I want to try.

"Thanks," Jason says. He even uses his spork instead of his fingers. That's smart. No Spam on his mango. Though actually Spam and mango together might be good. Spam and pineapple go good together.

I ask him if he's ever been to Disneyland. Then we argue about the best theme park. He says it's Knott's Berry Farm, which I've never heard of. I say it's the Six Flags in Arlington, Texas, because it's the first Six Flags. Even though I could only go on the kiddie rides when I was there.

Before we go back to class from lunch, Jason flips over the Polaroid and shows it to me. It's cool. The colors are kind of washed out, like we're looking through a dirty window. It makes it look haunted. Or old. He did a good job. The butterfly's wings are spread over the flower. I tell him it's good.

"Do you want it?" he asks. "I put all mine up on my wall."

"You took it, though," I say.

"It's okay," he says. "I can take more."

So I take the photo. I'll put it in my desk, with the other things I've collected. Tickets from museums and movies, doodles I did and liked, Mom's wristband from the hospital when she had Kaori. It'll fit well there.

"Do you take a lot of photos?" I ask.

"Yeah," Jason says. "Only film photos though. Mom says I'm an 'old soul.'"

"You could just use a phone," I say. "That's how we take all our pictures."

"I like not knowing exactly how it's going to look," Jason says. "It's a little surprise every time."

I kind of get that. A lot of times when I doodle, I don't have a plan. I just draw whatever comes to mind. It can turn into anything.

"Can I see your other pictures sometime?" I ask.

Jason's eyes go wide. "Really?" He smiles and ducks his head. "Yeah, duh. I'll bring some. Or maybe you can come over."

I haven't been invited to someone's house (outside of birthday parties when the birthday kid has obviously been forced to invite the whole class) in a long time. "Cool."

Jason grins at me. I can't help grinning back. It feels special. Like the moment in an anime when the robot fighters all come together to make one big robot. Our powers combining to make us even more awesome.

Toward the end of the week, Jason and I are sitting in our usual lunch spot when Mei comes over to us. She's wearing cherry-themed clothes today. "Come eat lunch with us," she says. "You look like losers over here."

"Maybe I like being a loser," I say to her.

Mei rolls her eyes. "Oh my god, just come sit." She grabs me by the arm and pulls me up. She's surprisingly strong. "Jason, come on."

"Um, okay," Jason says, eyes wide behind his glasses. He scrambles to his feet.

Mei brings us to her table. Kiana and Grace are both kind of frowny, but Mei acts like this is totally normal, sitting down and launching into a story about her new puppy. I talk about Mr. Knuckles and how he's doing at the house now that he's out of quarantine.

It's kind of awkward at first, especially because Kiana pulls out her phone to play some game. Jason recognizes it and asks her which character she likes. Kiana perks up at this. She turns her phone around and shows it to us. She's playing as a little girl with cat ears and a tail.

"She shoots ice arrows," Kiana explains. On-screen, her character yawns cutely. Video games are more E.J.'s thing, but I like the art.

"That's cool," I say.

After that everything seems to be a lot easier. We start talking about movies and TV—Mei likes *Sailor Moon*, but Grace and Kiana like reality shows—and complain about the school food. I feel like I've been powered with a brand-new battery. I can't stop talking. And none of them tell me to be quiet. I even make Mei laugh with my impression of Tuxedo Mask. They're more fun than I thought they'd be. And it's cool to have a group to talk to. I could get used to it.

INCIDENT REPORT

Date
Thursday, September 23

Location
Joe Takata Elementary

Event Description
My plan to make friends seems to be working. Today Mei invited me and Jason to eat lunch with her, Grace, and Kiana. Grace and Kiana are both local, not military, kids. They all go to the same church.

I thought Kiana seemed kind of stuck-up before. And Grace is one of those really well-behaved kids. Which is totally not me. And I guess I was right that Kiana is a little stuck-up, but it's more funny than mean. And Grace really is a Goody Two-shoes, but it's actually okay. She isn't the kind that tattles, she's just well behaved.

What surprised me was that they were super excited that I can draw. Kiana saw some of the drawings on my homework when it spilled out of my backpack. They got all excited and asked me to draw them, so I did. That really impressed them.

I didn't realize art could make people like me. It was cool to make people smile just by doodling cartoons of them. I liked it.

PERSONNEL FILE

Name
Ishida, Mei

Date of Birth
November 13

Place of Birth
Honolulu, Hawai'i

Place of Residence
Fort Shafter, Hawai'i

Occupation
Student

Primary Specialties
Acting, dressing up, inventing games

Awards and Citations
Classmate I Never Thought I'd Like but Actually She's Kinda Cool

Disciplinary Record
Probably none

Remarks
Mei is the oldest kid in her family too. She has two little brothers who are twins and are in first grade at our school. We bonded over annoying siblings, even though E.J. is a different kind of annoying. But there are some things all siblings do. Like shove their stuff into your space on car rides or repeat everything you say. Mei says she's lucky that her brothers are twins, because they spend most of their time together and don't follow her around all the time. E.J. followed me some when he was really small, but he stopped when he started reading.

SITUATION REPORT

Date
Wednesday, September 29

Location
Joe Takata Elementary

Activities Planned
Parents' Night presentation

Logistical Requirements
Finished report (typed up and everything)

Ketchup

Cupcakes (baked by Mom)

Sriracha

Obstacles Anticipated
Mom can't taste-test the cupcakes before we leave.

I'll have to carry the ketchup around the whole time.

Remarks
I still can't figure Mrs. Ashton out. Nothing seems to bother her. I implemented the plan I told Noah about and snuck in a jar of geckos I caught out in the parking lot. Right when she was starting to explain some math problem, I opened the jar. Everyone started yelling, even the boys. Ms. Nicole screamed so loud my ears rang.

But Mrs. Ashton just put down the whiteboard marker and went to the door. She opened it, put the little wedge underneath, then came back to the front. "They'll leave soon enough," she told everyone. "Don't mind them."

Then I tried messing with the xylophone. I folded up a piece of paper really small and wedged it under one of the keys so it couldn't vibrate when she hit it. When she played the xylophone for our independent study session, the only sound it made was a dull *thump*.

"I guess it's time to change up the tune," she said, and she played a different set of notes.

I think she knows it was me, but she hasn't done anything about it. I know Ms. Nicole wants me to get in trouble, because once or twice she's started to scold me before Mrs. Ashton interrupts. She never makes it seem like a real interruption, though. She asks Ms. Nicole for help or distracts her. Then she winks at me, like we're friends.

We aren't friends. Even if she doesn't make me join in reading *The Secret Garden* anymore.

At this point I'd rather she just get mad at me already. The longer she likes me, the angrier she'll be when I finally make her snap. And she will snap. Every teacher has. Sometimes it's something as simple as me failing my fifth spelling test in a row. Sometimes it's because I stuck a whoopee cushion on their chair. But it always happens.

I've been planning a new attack. One that will make her acknowledge that I'm a troublemaker. One that will make sure she knows that I can't be ignored. One that will prove that she doesn't know me half as well as she thinks she does.

15

PART OF OUR BIG RESEARCH PROJECT IS A PRESENTA-tion with a "creative interpretation" during Parents' Night. Mei is doing hers on the hula, so she's performing a dance. Jason's project is on Hanauma Bay. He has a bunch of really cool pictures of fish he took with an underwater camera and has put them together in a collage.

Mrs. Ashton was right, by the way. The story of James Cook's death is pretty interesting. I don't want to admit that to her, because I bet she'll be really smug. And I don't want her to think she knows me.

Most kids don't like speaking in front of other people. That's why Jason isn't doing a speaking presentation. Me? I love it. It's one of those times when it's good to have everyone's attention on you, because

they *have* to listen to what you say. I'm prepared. Jason, Mei, and I practiced my little play together in Mei's backyard.

And Mom's bringing cupcakes. Which is perfect.

It was her idea to bring something. Don't think I made her. She got the flyer for Parents' Night and told Dad that they should bring something for the class and teachers. I just suggested cupcakes when she asked what people might want. And I volunteered to help. Mom looked so surprised when I did. Little does she know.

The cupcakes are out of the oven right now. They smell amazing, like vanilla and butter. Mom made Funfetti cupcakes, which are the best. Now I just have to figure out how to get Mom out of the kitchen long enough to do my work.

This is where having a baby sister comes in handy. It would be easier if I could tell Kaori to start crying at a certain time, obviously, but I know her nap schedule. I messed around the kitchen to delay the baking a bit so that we'd go until Kaori wakes up from her afternoon nap. And right on cue, Kaori starts wailing.

"Aiya." Mom dusts her hands off on the kitchen towel and looks at me. "Can you frost these, Airi? Do it nicely, like I showed you."

"Of course," I tell her. She's too distracted to suspect me. Normally she would know right away something is up. I wait for her to go upstairs. Then I retrieve my secret weapon.

Sriracha.

I scoop out all the vanilla frosting into a big bowl. Then I take the bottle of sriracha and give it a big squeeze. I add a few drops of red food coloring to make it look good. I put the bottle back and mix up the frosting until it's a nice, pretty pink. Mom will like that. She'll think it's nice.

I start frosting the way Mom taught me. It's easy, but it makes the cupcakes look really nice. You use a spoon instead of a knife. Put a big scoop of frosting on top, then use the back of the spoon to swirl the frosting around until it comes to a nice soft-serve ice cream point. It kind of looks like Kaori's head when we wash her hair.

Mom made two dozen cupcakes. Not enough for everyone in my class and E.J.'s, but that's okay. I don't need everyone to eat one. Just Mrs. Ashton. Actually, I've already hinted to Jason and Mei that they shouldn't eat them unless they're feeling brave. So we'll see if they dare.

I carefully put the cupcakes in the two pans Mom is using to transport them. They look so pretty. I stick my finger into the remaining frosting in the bowl and give it a taste. *Awful.* Vanilla and sriracha don't go together at all. It's perfect.

When Mom comes downstairs holding Kaori, everything is done. I've even washed the bowl and the cupcake pan. Mom's so distracted with Kaori that she doesn't ask why I'm being so good. She's just glad, because there's so much to do before we leave. Dad doesn't have time to come home first, so he's going straight to the school. Mom has to get everything ready for when Cousin Layla comes over to babysit Kaori. She makes me and E.J. get dressed nicely, even though our teachers and classmates see us in normal clothes every day. She even brushes my hair and pulls it into a high ponytail, which hurts a little, but it does keep my hair out of my face.

PERSONNEL FILE

Name
Kim, Layla

Date of Birth
June 1

Place of Birth
Honolulu, Hawai'i

Place of Residence
Mililani, Hawai'i

Occupation
College student in marine biology at the University of Hawai'i

Primary Specialties
Surfing, making pizza from scratch

Awards and Citations
She's placed in a bunch of youth surfing competitions.

Disciplinary Record
Unknown (Mom doesn't like her tattoos, but I think they're neat.)

Remarks
We call her Cousin Layla, but her dad is actually Uncle Dan, Dad's best friend from high school. She's *so cool*. She's going to be an environmental lawyer, which she says is like being Earth's lawyer. Which kind of makes her like a superhero, in my opinion. She's promised to teach me to surf.

16

IT'S WEIRD TO GO TO THE SCHOOL AT NIGHT. EVERYTHING looks different. Kind of haunted. The classrooms all glow with lights. No one's running around or carrying backpacks. There's music coming from some of the rooms. I would like it if it weren't a school.

The fifth graders are doing their presentations first, so Mom takes half the cupcakes and E.J. to his class. That's fine by me. I take the other half of the cupcakes to Mrs. Ashton's class. I set them down on her desk and look around the classroom. Mrs. Ashton is talking to some parents. Ms. Nicole is straightening out one of the displays. I decide to scope out the competition.

A lot of the class did some kind of art for the creative part of their research project. Kai, the one who did his on Zippy's, created a diorama of one of their restaurants.

There's even a teeny-tiny plate of loco moco and a tiny bowl of saimin on one of the tables. It could have been made by the Menehune.[21] Jason put all the photos he took on a poster board. The best one is of a turtle that is looking right at the camera. Jason also put little captions underneath some of the photos. That one says, "Whooooaaaaa."

There's a lot of other neat stuff. Kiana made a whole bunch of leis from different things. There's even one that's made of plastic netting with money inside. The one made of plumeria smells so good. I stick my nose into it and take a big sniff.

SOME OF THE PARENTS' NIGHT PROJECTS I THOUGHT WERE INTERESTING

★ A copy of the statue of King Kamehameha made out of Lego

★ One of those baking soda volcanoes to represent Mount Kīlauea[22]

★ A hand-painted re-creation of the Obama HOPE poster from when he was first elected[23]

---

21 The Menehune are tiny forest people that supposedly lived in Hawai'i a super-long time ago. They built all kinds of stuff—roads, houses, boats, even temples! Dad says they could be as small as a phone standing on its end!

22 If you ask me, that isn't very creative since we all know how to make a baking soda volcano. But Brayden did make the volcano part look nice.

23 This was before I was born. Dad has a button with the picture on it.

- ⭐ A crocheted stuffed nēnē bird[24]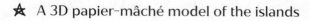
- ⭐ A 3D papier-mâché model of the islands
- ⭐ Mei's hula dance
- ⭐ Emma playing "Aloha 'Oe" on the ukulele
- ⭐ Zach demonstrating the proper stance for surfing
- ⭐ Wyatt showing a short video he took hiking up Diamond Head

Mom and Dad arrive from E.J.'s class in time to see the end of Mei's dance. I asked to go last when Mrs. Ashton was setting up the order. No one ever wants to go first or last when making presentations. It worked out too because it gave my parents time to get to my class. Besides, it wouldn't have been fair to everyone else if I'd gone first. Because I'm going to bring the house down. I can't wait. It's going to be amazing. I think it'll be fun for people who have a sense of humor. Who don't think that history has to be all serious all the time. And it's sure to make Mrs. Ashton mad, because I'm going to make a big mess.

For my creative presentation, I've decided to do a dramatic reenactment. At first I thought I might do a comic, but that wouldn't be shocking enough. I need to make a statement. Jason, Mei, and I have practiced. Jason wanted a script, but we don't need one. Not for this.

---

24 That's the state bird. It's a type of goose that's endangered. Mongooses like to eat it. This is why invasive species are bad. I like the nēnē bird because it's brave. It likes to live on volcanoes and golf courses. Isn't that so cool? It would be awesome to live on a volcano, as long as the lava didn't kill you.

THE STORY OF JAMES COOK: A JERK WHO GOT WHAT HE DESERVED

James Cook was born in England in 1728. He joined the British navy and did lots of military stuff in Canada during the Seven Years' War. He made the best maps of Newfoundland that had been made until then.

After that, he got sent to the Pacific Ocean to explore. He and his crew had to sail all the way around South America to get there. On his first trip, he went to Tahiti and then to New Zealand and Australia. He met Australians and wrote racist things about their skin color. Then he crashed his ship into the Great Barrier Reef. He decided that everything he saw belonged to England, even though people lived there already. On the way back to England, lots of his crew died from malaria, which they got from mosquitoes. The whole trip took three years, and it made him very famous.

For his next trip, he sailed south. People thought there was a big continent down there that kept the world balanced. It turns out they were right, and that was Antarctica, but Cook didn't find it. Instead he got into fights with the Māori, who are the native people of New Zealand, and claimed a bunch of other islands belonged to England. Back then, you could just sail to any place and say you owned it, and people believed you.

Cook's third trip was to look for a way from the Atlantic to the Pacific without having to go all the way around South America. He found Hawai'i instead, which he called the Sandwich Islands after the Earl of Sandwich, who was also the person to invent the sandwich.

The first island he visited was Kaua'i. The Hawaiians were very nice to him. They traded food for iron and exchanged knowledge. After that, he spent a year exploring the western coast of the mainland. He met the Yuquot people in Vancouver and was annoyed because he couldn't trade worthless junk to them like he did in Hawai'i. This continued a pattern of Cook having bad relations with the native people wherever he went.

Cook went all the way to Alaska, then to the coast of Siberia. He began to act weirdly and made his crew eat gross walrus meat. He spotted the same island four times in one day and named it differently each time. He would get angry really suddenly, which people call "fits of rage" but is just a grown-up version of a tantrum.

Cook returned to Hawai'i, this time landing at Kealakekua Bay on the Big Island. People say that the Hawaiians thought he was a god because he arrived during the Makahiki festival for the god Lono and they also called him Lono. But some people say that Lono was a nickname for highly respected people, but it doesn't mean they thought he was a god.

Even if they didn't think he was a god, Cook was treated very nicely. The priests included him in rituals. The Hawaiians traded lots of supplies, and their king, Kalani'opu'u, came to the bay to meet Cook. Kalani'opu'u and Cook exchanged tokens of friendship. Cook was treated as a fellow chief and was given great respect. Cook and his sailors stayed for one month while they fixed their ship.

When Cook's crew tried to leave, they ran into a big storm that damaged their ship again. They returned to the Big Island. This time they weren't greeted with a big happy crowd. The Hawaiians were tired of Cook by then, and they didn't want to share more food because there was a war going on between the Big Island and Mauʻi. But they wanted iron to make weapons. They wanted it so bad they stole tools from the ship. They also took one of Cook's sailboats so they could take out its nails.

This made Cook very mad. He decided that he was going to take Kalaniʻopuʻu hostage until the sailboat was returned. When Cook took him, the Hawaiians followed because they were worried about their king. A fight broke out when the Hawaiians tried to protect their king. Cook fired his gun and killed a Hawaiian man. Then the Hawaiians pushed Cook into the sand and stabbed him. The Hawaiians and the sailors fought until the sailors had to retreat to their ship.

The sailors took revenge by killing some Hawaiians. Meanwhile, the Hawaiians had taken Cook's body for ceremonial burial. Even though he had tried to kidnap their king, they treated him respectfully. His body was ritually cut up and burned, and his bones were given to different chiefs. Later they gave some bones to the sailors to bury out of respect for their traditions.

Cook's ship finally left a week later. But that wasn't the end of Cook's effect on Hawaiʻi. Now England knew where Hawaiʻi was, and that meant more haoles came. Also, for many years people believed a lie about the Hawaiians eating Cook's body. This rumor was from racist people who wanted to make the Hawaiians seem like animals. Though if they had eaten Cook, he would have deserved it because of his lack of respect for the people he met. Overall the Hawaiian people would probably be happier if Cook had never found them.

I play James Cook. Jason plays the Hawaiian king. Mei plays the man who killed James Cook. I had to bribe them with Pocky to get them to do it, but Mei actually likes acting. I had Jason be the king because he doesn't have to say much. He just has to let me lead him to the front of the classroom and then say, "I don't want to go anymore. Where are you taking me?"

"I will hold you on my ship until your people return the things they stole!" I say.

Jason sits down on the floor. "I won't go."

Mei marches up the aisle to the front of the classroom, waving a wrapping-paper tube. "Where are you taking our king?" she shouts. She's really into it. She was really excited when I told her that we would fake sword-fight. She's a lot more bloodthirsty than she looks.

"Your king must answer for your crimes!" I tell her.

"You've broken the bonds of friendship and disrespected our traditions." Mei puts her hand on her hip. "For that, you must be punished!"

"I am a god to you!" I shout.

"You're no god of mine!" Mei yells back.

Then we fight with the wrapping-paper tubes. James Cook actually had a gun, but that wouldn't be as interesting to watch. So we fence, and then I fall dramatically to the ground. Mei stands over me, laughing like a supervillain.

"And that's what you get!" she says. "Death to the invaders!"

She stabs down at me with her tube. This is the best part. The part I've been waiting for.

Under my shirt I have a bottle of ketchup I took from the refrigerator at home. I snuck it in with the cupcakes. Mom had no idea. I have it between my ribs and my elbow. I squeeze as hard as I can and yell at the top of my lungs.

The ketchup comes shooting out. It goes *everywhere*. Some even hits the ceiling. Mei gets some on her face and wipes it off and eats it. I keep squeezing until the ketchup stops coming out. Then I flop down flat on the floor and close my eyes.

"Muahaha!" Mei puts her foot on my chest. "And now we are free from the haoles!"

We give it a moment. You have to let everyone take in the scene. And then I jump to my feet and say, "And that's how James Cook died!"

There's ketchup all over the front row of desks. Some got on the parents. A few of them look pretty mad. Whoops! But I don't care. Because it was exactly how I imagined it. Maybe a little messier than I thought, but that's even better. I wanted drama. I wanted excitement. And I wanted people to never forget my performance. I'm pretty sure we nailed it.

I grab Mei's hand and pull Jason up, and we bow. From the back of the classroom, I hear my dad laugh and then start clapping. I straighten up and give him a big grin. He grins back. Mom has her arms crossed. Oh well. I knew she wouldn't like it. She doesn't like it when I "make a scene."

Mrs. Ashton is clapping too. She's actually smiling, super big. And it seems sincere. I can't believe her. Is she for real?

"Bravo, Airi!" she says. "That was very vivid!"

"Oh my god," Ms. Nicole says. She looks horrified. "There's so much to clean up . . ."

"Sorry," I say to Mei and Jason. I didn't tell them about

the ketchup. I wanted it to be a surprise. Also, they might have stopped me. I hope they aren't mad. "You don't have to help clean."

"That was *awesome*," Mei says, her eyes wide. I'm starting to realize she's a lot cooler than I thought.

"I think I got ketchup in my hair," Jason says. He pokes his finger into his curls.

To my surprise, Jason and Mei volunteer to help me clean up. They wipe off the desks and the floor. I have to do the ceiling. I have to stand on a desk to reach, and even then I have to use a broom to rub the cloth against the ketchup. But it was totally worth it. Even if Mom is watching me and pointing out spots I missed.

When I get down, Mrs. Ashton comes over to me and my parents. "That was a very unique presentation, Airi," she says. "Very memorable. I don't know how anyone will ever be able to top it."

"You inspired me," I say, with my most angelic face. "My mom and I even made those cupcakes for you." I point at her desk.

"I was wondering where those were from!" Mrs. Ashton turns to my mom. "Thank you, Mrs. Sano."

"It is no trouble at all," Mom says.

"I know Airi can be a handful," Dad says. "Are you doing all right with her?"

"Hey!" I say.

Mrs. Ashton smiles and winks at me. "Not at all. Airi is a joy to have in class."

"You should try one," I tell Mrs. Ashton. "I frosted them myself."

Mom looks at me, frowning slightly. Now she's suspicious. But she won't say anything in front of Mrs. Ashton. So there's no one to stop Mrs. Ashton from picking up the tray of cupcakes and offering it to Ms. Nicole. Some of the kids take them too, and a few of the parents. Soon all of the cupcakes have been handed out except one. Mrs. Ashton's cupcake.

I watch everyone closely. Ms. Nicole bites into hers and makes a face. She holds it up like she thinks there's a trick inside. Jake takes a huge chomp and starts coughing right away, his eyes tearing up. His dad scolds him for eating too quickly while Jake runs to the trash can to spit out his mouthful. I look back at Mrs. Ashton and smile.

"Airi, what did you do?" Mom asks under her breath in Japanese. It's too late, though. Mrs. Ashton has already unwrapped the last cupcake and brought it to her mouth. I hold my breath. Here it is. Here's the moment she's going to finally admit that I'm a troublemaker. And she'll finally leave me alone.

Mrs. Ashton takes a dainty bite. Her face doesn't change at all. She chews, swallows, and takes another bite. My eyes widen.

A second bite?!

She swallows the second bite. "That's a very unique flavor," Mrs. Ashton says. "Spicy and sweet isn't for everyone, but it's very gourmet. Where did you get the idea?"

"Spicy?" Mom asks.

"Do you . . . like it?" I ask. This makes no sense. Are Mrs. Ashton's taste buds broken?

"Hmm, I think I would change the recipe a bit for the next time," Mrs. Ashton says. "I think you need a savory element, like some candied bacon on top. And you might want to change the frosting from vanilla to a plain cream cheese frosting."

She's actually giving me tips on how to do this again? That's it. She's not normal. She can't be.

Mom's jaw is very tense. Her mouth is pressed into that thin line she gets when she's mad and doesn't want to show it. Dad looks like he can't decide if he wants to laugh or sigh. Mrs. Ashton takes *another bite*.

I open my mouth to ask again if she likes it, because I just can't believe it. But Dad taps me on the shoulder. "Airi," he says, "could you go get your brother from his class so we can talk to Mrs. Ashton for a minute?"

"Fine," I say, and I turn around and march out of the room. My stomach is all clenched up. Because when my parents want to talk to my teacher, it usually means I'm going to be in trouble. Mrs. Ashton has been nice to me, but what teachers really care about is the parents. Keeping the parents happy is more important than if the kid is happy. That's why they invented grades.

E.J. is hanging out with some of his friends. He already has a whole group of them. E.J. has always been good at making friends. Everywhere we go he has a group. He even keeps in touch with them after we move. They play games online together. It doesn't seem fair, because E.J. is good at school too. He shouldn't get to have both. He doesn't even need to study that much—he just learns things and remembers them.

"Hey," I say to him. "Eiji."

He turns and scowls at me. He hates when I call him by his full name. "What?"

"Mom and Dad want to go soon," I say. "Come on."

"Hi," says one of E.J.'s friends. She has lots of braids and cat-eye glasses. "I didn't know E.J. had a sister."

"I go here too," I say. "So you'd better watch out."

"Jesus Christ, Airi," E.J. says.

"You sound like Mrs. Forsythe," I say. Mrs. Forsythe was our neighbor back in Kentucky. She babysat us when Mom and Dad were doing stuff at the hospital for Mom's pregnancy with Kaori, even though I think I'm old enough to watch E.J. Her favorite thing to say was "Jesus Christ, Airi," with her big Southern twang. There was one time when she was asking how my summer reading was going, so I showed her my copy of *Holes* that I'd carved holes into. They were all different depths and sizes. I thought it was clever. She was horrified. I think she doesn't appreciate art.

"Whatever." E.J. pushes his glasses up his nose. "Why do you have ketchup in your hair?"

"You wouldn't understand," I tell him. "Geniuses are never truly understood in their lifetime."

E.J. scoffs. "You're *far* from a genius."

Which is just rude. I grab him by the ear—I've seen Grandma do this to Dad—and drag him yelling from the room.

He's still complaining when we get to Mrs. Ashton's room, even though I've let go of his ear. When Mom sees us, she just sighs. Dad comes over to ruffle E.J.'s hair and asks if I'm being mean to him. But he winks at me when he says it. He knows I would never *really* hurt E.J. And E.J. just makes a face anyway.

"We'd better head out," Dad says. "Thank you again, Mrs. Ashton. It was really nice to meet you."

"You as well!" Mrs. Ashton gives me a smile. "I'll see you in class tomorrow, Airi."

I do *not* understand her. "You betcha." I give her finger-guns.

Mom gives Mrs. Ashton a little bow, the way she does

when she forgets she isn't in Japan. It's so embarrassing. "Please let us know what you decide."

"What does that mean?" I ask.

Mom doesn't answer. She takes my arm and starts leading me out of the room. I twist around to look back at Mrs. Ashton, but she's still smiling. Which is weird, because "decisions" usually mean that I'm in trouble. And people don't smile at someone they're going to punish unless they're really evil. I don't think Mrs. Ashton is evil. Eva's too nice for that.

When we get home, Mom and Dad pay Cousin Layla, who gives me a big hug and E.J. a fist bump before leaving. Then Mom and Dad send E.J. up to his room. But they tell me to stay.

"We need to talk to you," Dad says. He leads the way into the living room. I take the big armchair. Mom and Dad sit on the couch. Which I realize is bad, because now they're both looking at me with serious expressions. Great. Guess I really am in trouble.

"I don't think it was so bad," I say right away, before they can even start talking. "I only put some sriracha in the frosting."

"*That's* what you did?" Dad shakes his head, smiling a little. That's good. He's not too mad yet. "I guess it could be worse."

Mom gives Dad an annoyed look. "Airi, why on earth would you do such a thing?"

I shrug. "I thought it would be funny. And it was."

"I wanted to do something *nice* for your teacher," Mom says. Her brow is furrowing deeper and deeper. "I thought I could *trust* you with—never mind." She takes a breath and closes her eyes briefly. "It isn't the cupcakes."

"Oh." I try to think what else it could be. "I can pay for the bottle of ketchup I used up. I still have money from mowing Mrs. Forsythe's lawn."

"Not that either," Dad says. "Though I have to say, I thoroughly enjoyed your performance. Who knew we had an actress in the family?"

"Airi is very good at acting," Mom says. I feel like she doesn't mean that in a good way.

"Okay," I say. "What is it?"

If it isn't about tonight, it must be about the pranks I've been pulling at school. And sure enough, Dad says, "Mrs. Ashton has some concerns she wants us to discuss with you."

Here it is. Mrs. Ashton must have asked them to punish me for her. That's creative. My other teachers never figured out that I didn't mind their punishments that much. Getting sent to the office or being put out in the hall is boring, but I can nap or doodle if I'm able to sneak a pencil or pen away.

I have a pair of sneakers that I've drawn all over. They're my favorite.

I'm too old for Mom to put me in a corner like she used to. She's wised up to my tricks. Now she'll take away my comics or my art supplies, or she'll sit and watch me do my home-work so I can't slack off. Now that Kaori doesn't sleep as much as she did when she was first born, Mom hasn't had as much time to keep an eye on me. Which has been great.

But this time Dad's involved. He doesn't care about the same things as Mom, but when he's upset with me, it's the worst. His voice gets really quiet and serious, and he stops smiling. He looks at me all disappointed. I've gotten used to disappointing Mom. I *hate* disappointing Dad.

I wait for it. I wonder which one it was. I bet it was the geckos.

Then Dad says, "Mrs. Ashton told us you've been having some trouble with reading."

I freeze. My entire body feels hot and cold at the same time. This is wrong. Why would she tell them that? "That isn't true," I say.

"Airi, it's okay," Dad says. "It's no big deal. She wants to work with you to find strategies to manage it."

"There's nothing to *manage*," I say. "I read just fine. You see how many comic books I have."

"That's what I said!" Dad smiles at me. I hate it. I never thought I'd hate Dad's smile. "Mrs. Ashton thinks that you're able to process visual narrative better than text, but she'd like to do some more tests. There's an educational-needs class that you can take . . ."

All of these words are too much. I can't listen. I'm think-ing about how nice Mrs. Ashton has been about not making me read aloud. I thought maybe it was because of the speech

I gave on why the book is bad. Was she taking pity on me? Well, I don't *need* it.

"I'm not stupid!" I say loudly, interrupting Dad in the middle of his sentence. Mr. Knuckles, who was sleeping on the back of the couch, wakes up and yowls. "I can't believe she told you that!" My face is hot. Now I know why they sent E.J. upstairs. They want to help me "save face." Perfect E.J. and his perfect grades.

"Airi, no one is saying you're stupid," Dad says.

"Then why do I have to go to a special class?" I demand. "I don't *want* to be in a special class! I don't want to take *tests*."

"Airi," Mom sighs. "Please don't yell. Mrs. Ashton says if you want, she can work with you one-on-one . . ."

I slump back in my seat and cross my arms tight over my chest. I think about Mrs. Ashton playing word games with me or asking me to spell things. About her letting me use video sources for my project. I thought she was weird. But this whole time she's been testing me and my reading.

Which I do fine. I know lots of words. I have them fully memorized. Just because sometimes I can't figure out what one means or how to say it doesn't mean I can't read. No one was supposed to notice, or care. No one has before. Now I'm being singled out.

Mom is still talking. I only hear the last part of what she's saying. "—just don't understand why you never told us you were having trouble. We could have helped you."

"There's nothing for you to know. And English isn't even your first language," I say to her. "How are you supposed to help me?"

Mom's mouth snaps shut. She crosses her arms. The little fold between her eyebrows gets even deeper. Dad gives me a disappointed look, his face becoming very serious. I've only seen him look that way when he's really upset.

"Airi, apologize to your mom," Dad says sternly. "That was completely uncalled for."

I look down at my hands. It feels like someone scooped out my stomach with a spoon and dropped a big rotten coconut inside. I don't know why I said it. "Sorry," I mutter.

"You'll have to do better than that," Dad says.

"No." Mom gets up. "It's fine. I will go to bed now."

I don't look up until I hear Mom's footsteps going up the stairs. Then I peek up at Dad. He's still looking at me with that disappointed look. It makes me feel all squirmy inside, like something wormy and awful is trying to escape.

"Airi," he says, "that was a very mean thing to say to your mother."

I don't say anything.

"Why would you say something like that?"

"I don't know," I mumble.

Dad heaves a great big sigh and stands up. "You know I love you very much, right?" I nod. He comes up to me and rests his hand on top of my head. "I just wish you would think a little more about how what you do affects others. I think your heart is usually in the right place, but sometimes . . ."

He doesn't finish his thought. Which is worse than if he did. Now I'm just thinking of all the things he might have said. Sometimes I make him so mad. Sometimes he hates me a little. Sometimes I'm as evil as a supervillain.

He leaves me alone after reminding me not to go to bed too late. I flip through the channels on TV for a while before giving up and just watching the channel guide. I like watching it scroll by with the ukulele music in the background. It's hypnotizing.

I go up to bed after watching the guide scroll through twice. As I tiptoe past Mom and Dad's room, I catch a glimpse of them inside. Dad is holding Mom in his arms and talking quietly. My whole chest aches when I see it.

To make myself feel better, I peek in on Kaori. She's sleeping peacefully all bundled up tight. She's holding on to the ear of a stuffed bunny. I love the way her little cheeks look. Her little eyelashes. I reach down and gently tuck away her wispy hair. Then I go to my room and lie in bed listening to sad Asian drama theme songs until I fall asleep.

AFTER ACTION REPORT

Date
Wednesday, September 29

Location
Joe Takata Elementary

Actions Undertaken
Parents' Night presentation

Duration
Two hours

Purpose
Putting on a good show

Finally making Mrs. Ashton mad

Mission Result
Complete failure

Remarks
I didn't learn to read until I was in first grade. Then I started memorizing the way words and sounds and meanings went together, and things got easier. I still don't like it. It takes too long. I could just watch something or read a comic book. That doesn't mean I can't read. Or that I have reading problems.

I got Mrs. Ashton all wrong. She's one of those teachers who thinks she can help me. I had a school counselor like that back in Kentucky. She had me draw a lot to "get out my feelings." Those kinds of adults always think they know everything. They think they know ME. Well, they don't. I can still take them by surprise. Like when I hid all the marker caps. Or when I put some food coloring in my pocket and pretended I'd cut my leg so I could leave and go to the nurse's office.

But I don't need help. I definitely don't need Mrs. Ashton's help. This just proves she isn't my friend.

I'M NOT LOOKING FORWARD TO SCHOOL TODAY. NOT
that I'm ever looking forward to school. But I'm especially
not today. I don't know what I'm going to do when I see Mrs.
Ashton. I'm so mad at her. I keep thinking of what I'm going
to say.

"I am not stupid!"

"Reading is for nerds anyway!"

"I want a different teacher!"

"I challenge you to a duel of honor!"

I get to class ready to tell her just what I think. I drop my
backpack at my desk. Then I stop. There's an envelope on
my seat. My name is written on it in swirly, curly writing.

There's only one person it could be from. I think about
throwing it away, *while* she's watching. Honestly, though, I'm
curious. What could she possibly want to say to me? Is it

to tell me formally that I need to go to a special class? Or maybe she wants to gloat. I have to say, telling my parents that I can't read is a strong move. She gets to punish me without punishing me. Again.

I rip open the envelope and sit down. Inside she has written in neat, very even letters. It says:

Airi,

It's hard to believe you've been in my class for only three weeks! You have brought so much fun and joy to our little room. Your play last night was wonderful! Very creative and funny!

You actually remind me of myself. I was a big prankster too, if you can believe it! I was even voted Best Prankster in the sixth grade. I bet I could have given you a run for your money.

Keep up the great work! I look forward to working with you the rest of this year.

Hattie Ashton

There's even an old-school photo of a girl about my age who looks a bit like Mrs. Ashton. She has the same hair (without the gray streaks) and the same smile. She even has almost the same glasses, just in brown. When I look on the back, it says *Harriet Ashton*.

I look in the envelope again, then

turn it upside down and shake it. Nothing else comes out. And there's nothing written inside or on the back of the card. No "Just kidding!" or "Haha, got you!" Which can't be right. No teacher has ever said it's *nice* to have me in class. That's the opposite of what I want.

There must be a trick somewhere. I look over to Mrs. Ashton. She's not looking at me, though. She's shuffling papers on her desk like nothing's wrong.

"Very clever," I mutter under my breath. "But I'll figure out your game."

Mei turns around and frowns at me. "What?"

"Nothing." I quickly shove the card into my backpack so she doesn't see. "Talking to myself."

Mei rolls her eyes. "You're so *weird*," she says. But she doesn't say it like it's a bad thing. Almost as though she likes that I'm weird.

I pay more attention in class than I ever have before. Not to the lesson. That's boring. No, I'm paying attention to Mrs. Ashton. Keeping an eye on if she's planning anything. She must be.

But she doesn't call on me once. She only looks at me a normal amount. It's almost like last night never happened at all. The only way you can tell is the red stains still on the ceiling. I guess I didn't scrub as good as I thought.

When recess is called, I go up to Mrs. Ashton. I bring the photo with me. I hold it up with the back facing her.

"I thought your name was Hattie," I say.

"It's short for Harriet." Mrs. Ashton makes a face, like

a little kid. "I never liked it. Everyone has always called me Hattie. Only my wife calls me Harriet, and that's just when she's mad at me."

I cross my arms. She can't distract me from my mission. "I'm not going to a special class," I say. "I don't need it."

"That's perfectly fine," Mrs. Ashton says calmly. "I happen to agree."

I pause. "What?"

"The normal course of action would be to pull you out three times a week for special education," Mrs. Ashton says. My stomach churns at the idea of all my classmates staring as I get up when they're about to start a lesson and leave to go to my weirdo lessons. "But I think you'd do better with the stability of one class." Mrs. Ashton leans forward and props her elbows on her desk. "And I have a few ideas about how to make learning a little easier for you."

"Who says I want to learn?" I demand. "I'm perfectly fine the way I am."

"That's true," she agrees. "How about this—we'll find some ways to make class more *fun*."

I scoff. "As if a grown-up could know what fun is. Besides, everyone knows that learning isn't fun."

Mrs. Ashton laughs. "Is that what you think? Remember, I was the best prankster when I was in middle school!"

"I'm sure you think you were," I say. "But that was *ages* ago. Like, probably fifty years ago."

Mrs. Ashton laughs. No, she *guffaws*. Not the delicate little tinkly laugh I'm used to. A full big-belly laugh. "Not quite that long ago," she says, after she stops laughing. "But I take your point. Maybe I've gotten rusty."

"I bet you have," I say. "You haven't even tried to stop my pranks."

"Those?" Mrs. Ashton waves her hand. "If you want to ruffle *my* feathers, Airi, you're going to have to try a little harder than that."

That sounds like a challenge. No, not a challenge. A declaration of war. A prank war.

I smile evilly. "Oh," I say, "I will."

Mrs. Ashton has no idea what's coming.

If I'm going to battle Mrs. Ashton on the field of pranks, I'm going to need a plan. I can't go at it like I have been, just doing things when I think of them. That might have worked in the past, but Mrs. Ashton has proved she's made of stronger stuff than my other teachers. Luckily, I'm an expert.

Dad's role in the military is in operations, which is all about planning and strategy. His department makes sure that everyone has the information they need and the supplies they want. Success depends on organization. That's what he's always taught me. So once I get home, I run upstairs to my desk, take out a notebook, and start writing my plans.

First: identify your goals. That's easy. My goal is to make Mrs. Ashton admit that I'm the superior prankster. Also, if possible, convince her to give up on trying to make learning "fun" for me, because that's just a waste of everyone's time.

Second: gather information. What do I know about Mrs. Ashton? I write the following in my notebook:

1. Her real name is Harriet, but she hates that name.

2. She has a daughter named Eva.

3. She's married.

4. She believes in ghosts.

Third: plan actual actions.

I start scribbling ideas for my three-part plan. The first part is pretty easy, but it's going to get complicated after that. I'll start with a warning shot across the bow. Just to let her know that I've accepted her challenge.

But what to target? She didn't care when I disrupted class. Even the geckos didn't bother her. I tap my pen against my lip. Then it comes to me. What do teachers love more than anything? Homework! I'll have to find a way to disrupt homework.

And it can't be just me. I'll have to gather allies. Jason and Mei will help. I might have to bribe them, but I'm sure I can get them on my side. And if all of us are in on it, what is Mrs. Ashton going to do? Punish all of us? That's collective action.[25]

Once I've let Mrs. Ashton know that it's on, it will be time

---

25 This is something Aunty Jen says a lot when a group of people protest something together. She's part of a union, which she says is collective action too. She says people working together get more work done than people working alone.

for part two: disrupt her peace of mind. I have to get her to lose that calm. This might take a few different pranks. But I'm ready for it.

Last is to completely upend her environment. Teachers hate a mess. And Mrs. Ashton's room is carefully put together. She has the papasan, and the bookshelf, and all the nice posters and pictures on the wall. If I've learned anything from *The Sims*, it's that messing with a room can seriously affect someone's mood. Then, once she's off-balance, I'll deliver the final blow. I don't know exactly how I'll do it just yet. Whatever I do, I'll need help.

I sit back and look over my notes. I wish I could write in code. Then this would be even more top secret. But Mom says my handwriting is impossible to read anyway. So I doubt anyone will be able to figure out what I'm doing even if they find the notes.

I go down for dinner, running through the different things I could do to Mrs. Ashton. Dad has picked up food from L&L. I have fried shrimp and rice. Dad always gets the lau lau and kalua pork. Mom has barbecue chicken because she's boring. E.J. always has the loco moco. He's so predictable. He gets that *everywhere*.

lau lau (l-ow l-ow): This looks like a big mess when you see it, because it's meat wrapped in taro leaves and then steamed. The leaves get all slimy and wet. If you go to one of the touristy luaus, they'll serve you traditional lau lau that they bury underground on hot rocks.

 **loco moco** (LOH-koh MOH-koh): The funny thing is that this means "crazy snot" in Spanish! But it's actually a big plate of food. You layer rice, gravy, a hamburger patty, and a fried egg and dig in. E.J. likes fried Spam in his too.

We're finishing up eating when Dad sets down his chopsticks and says, "There's a possibility I might be going to Guam for a few months."

All of us stop what we're doing and turn to look at him. Even Kaori, whose face is covered in Mom's homemade squash oyaki, turns her head. Mom's hand is shaking as she puts down her glass of water. It feels as though the shrimp in my stomach have come back to life and are trying to wriggle out of me. My hands start to sweat. I think I'm mad. Or I'm about to cry. It's hard to tell. My chest is all tight like I'm sad, but I'm hot all over too.

"When?" Mom asks.

"Not sure yet," Dad says. "They haven't decided. But they'd like me to spend some time at the bases there and help train staff."

"That is a very big honor," Mom says. She doesn't sound like she means it. "How long would it be?"

"Four to six months," Dad says. "With leave so I can come home to visit, of course." Like that makes it any better.

"No," I say loudly.

Dad looks at me. "Airi—"

"No." I stand up, shoving my chair back from the table. "That's ridiculous. You have to tell them no."

"I understand," Mom says to Dad quietly. "How certain is it?"

"Who cares about orders?" I demand. "There are other people they can send. They don't need Dad."

Kaori is looking around at us with big eyes. She doesn't like yelling. But I can't help it. There's just too much, and it all wants to come bursting out. How could the army do this? They promised Dad. He promised *us*. I can't even imagine how Mom feels. She was already so unhappy when she was pregnant and he was away a lot. Now he's going to just leave?

"What about Kaori?" I ask. "You'll miss her first birthday."

"Airi, I can't just turn them down," Dad says wearily.

"Then the army is wrong. You shouldn't have to just *do* everything they say." I look at E.J. "Aren't you gonna say anything?"

E.J. shrugs. "Shikata ga nai,"[26] he says. He looks down at his plate and pokes his chopsticks in the last bit of mac salad.

"Don't just copy Mom," I snap. "You're *such* a little suck-up. Don't you think for yourself?" I glare around the table. Dad looks very serious, but not like he's thinking about changing his mind. Mom has her usual tight-lip expression. E.J. just seems like he doesn't care at all.

Kaori starts crying. Mom sighs and gets up to soothe her. "Airi, please," she says. "Stop yelling."

My eyes are hot and prickly. Which means I'm about to cry, and I *won't*. I'm mad. I don't want them to try to comfort me. This is all their fault. The whole point of us moving

---

26 仕方がない, pronounced she-KAH-tah gah nye. I *hate* this phrase. It means something like "It can't be helped" or "That's the way things are and you have to accept it." Mom always uses it when I complain about things. She wants me to just be emotionless and calm about everything. Like E.J.

to Hawai'i was supposed to be that Dad would be around more. We haven't even been here two months and Dad's already talking about going.

"Fine," I say. "I'll go somewhere so I can't bother you!"

I run upstairs rather than sit there and listen to them try to explain. I slam the door to my room shut, even though I know Mom and Dad hate that. Mr. Knuckles has curled up on the lower bunk, so I pick him up and press my face into his fur. He yowls and tries to wiggle away, but I squeeze him tighter. He actually likes that. He doesn't mind when I hold on.

Eventually Mr. Knuckles gets impatient and wiggles out of my arms. I watch him jump down from the bed and circle my pile of clothes on the floor before going to the door. I should let him out. But I feel too heavy to move.

It was supposed to be better here. Different. But everything is repeating. The only real differences are Mrs. Ashton, who might be terrible but is at least a new kind of challenge, and my new friends, who I'm actually really starting to like. And now I'm wondering what's even the point. If Dad's being sent away, who says they won't decide to make us move again?

So if I'm going to battle Mrs. Ashton, I better get started. There's no time to waste.

PERSONNEL FILE

Name
Ashton, Harriet, aka Hattie

Date of Birth
UNKNOWN

Place of Birth
UNKNOWN

Place of Residence
O'ahu, Hawai'i (I still don't know if her wife is in the military, so I'm not sure if she lives on base)

Occupation
Sixth-grade teacher

Primary Specialties
Speaking very softly, tricking people into taking tests, eating weird foods, pranks (or so she claims)

Awards and Citations
Best Prankster, sixth grade (or so she says); anything more recent is unknown

Disciplinary Record
UNKNOWN

Remarks
I still don't know much about her. I know she believes in ghosts and has a daughter named Eva. I have some ideas for ghost pranks, but they're all pretty complicated. I might have to put those aside for right now.

SITUATION REPORT

Date
Monday, October 4

Location
Joe Takata Elementary

Activities Planned
Opening shot of the prank war

Logistical Requirements
Sharpie

Wite-Out

Obstacles Anticipated
I need a distraction.

Remarks
I'll only have a few minutes to get this done. I can't afford any mistakes.

I START MY OFFENSIVE BRIGHT AND EARLY ON MONDAY.
The first step is to get an accomplice. For this, I pick Jason. He's shy and a little nervous, but that makes him perfect. No one would ever suspect him of playing a trick. And he doesn't even have to do that much. I just need a distraction.

At first, Jason doesn't want to help. He's suspicious. I think it's because of the ketchup he got on his face. He doesn't like being surprised like that. But I promise he doesn't have to do much. He just has to ask Mrs. Ashton for help during recess.

"Maybe ask her for a book recommendation," I say. "Or ask if she'll look at something for you. As long as she's away from her desk for a few minutes."

Jason still looks skeptical. But he agrees when I swear that it only involves our homework. Nothing else.

We make our move at recess. Mrs. Ashton is predictable.

Every Monday she gives us a packet for the week. The first page outlines what we're talking about in social studies and related topics from other subjects. After that are worksheets for each day. To "refresh what we've learned." Mrs. Ashton checks them at the end of the week.

She keeps the packet on her desk until lunch, when she gives it to Ms. Nicole to make copies. I've sat in enough school offices to know how copiers work. Teachers put the packet in all at once without looking at it, and it spits the copies out stapled. So if someone, for example, makes a few changes to the inside of the packet, it won't be noticed.

I came prepared. Wite-Out tape and a Sharpie. I even practiced at home.

I wait until Jason has gotten Mrs. Ashton's attention. He gets her over toward the door, her back to her desk. I sidle over, Wite-Out and pen in hand. Sure enough, there's the packet, sitting right next to her attendance sheet. Mrs. Ashton keeps her desk nice and tidy. Big mistake. If you keep things organized, it's easy for people to know where you keep things. That makes it easy to steal, or to sabotage. People are always telling me that if I were more organized and put things away, I wouldn't lose things as often. But I don't consider anything really lost. I know where I keep things. Organized chaos. And no one else knows how to find anything in my stuff. Which is just the way I like it.

It doesn't take me more than a few

minutes to do what I need. When I'm finished, I go back to my desk and pretend like I've been checking my homework. I whistle to let Jason know I'm finished. He looks over, and I give him a thumbs-up. Mission complete.

For the rest of the day, I watch Ms. Nicole and Mrs. Ashton. But they don't seem to notice anything. As usual, Mrs. Ashton gives Ms. Nicole the packet. After lunch, Ms. Nicole returns with the stack. They hand them out. And no one notices a thing.

The only problem with this prank is that it's going to take a week to pay off. In the meantime I have to play it cool. Pretend that I've decided to be good and obedient. I might even have to do some work in class to throw her off.

My chance comes the next day. Mrs. Ashton wants volunteers to come to the board and demonstrate some of the word problems in our math book. Even though I hate math, I raise my hand. It's necessary for the plan. I have to seem like an eager student. Make her think she's finally won me over. Ugh. The sacrifices I make for my art.

Lily does her word problem fast. She's the best at math in the class. Then Wyatt does his. He takes longer and keeps erasing his work on the whiteboard, then writing it again. But he eventually gets it right. Mrs. Ashton praises him for keeping at it. Now it's my turn.

I look at the question in the book. It shows a little white girl with a thinking bubble that says, *I have to wrap 25 gifts and I have 20 yards of ribbon. How many feet of ribbon do I have for each box?*

I wish I had read the question before volunteering. I have no idea what this means. I see the numbers, and I understand those. So I write *25* and *20* on the board. Then I stop and read the question again.

Hesitantly, I write *gifts* under *25*. I'm so nervous I mix up the "t" and "f" at first. My face gets hot as I use my fingers to wipe them away and write them again. The class is very quiet. I almost wish they were laughing at me instead. I don't like this. I can feel everyone watching me. Expecting.

What else do I know? There are three feet in a yard. That I know. I write that on the board: *3 feet = 1 yard.*

I stop again. I don't know where to go from here. The words swim in my eyes. Why don't they write simpler questions? I hate math writers.

"Airi," Mrs. Ashton says in her gentle voice. I clench my hand around the whiteboard marker. "Let's break this down into steps."

"I don't need your help," I snap. I turn my back to her.

Ribbon. Twenty yards of ribbon. What does that mean? I have to break it down on the board. I write *20, 20, 20.* I take a breath. This is better. 2 + 2 + 2 = 6. Then I just keep the O.

Sixty. Sixty feet of ribbon.

My heart is beating so hard I can't think. My sweaty hand slips on the marker. Twenty-five gifts. Sixty feet of ribbon. I know this is supposed to be pretty easy. But I don't know where to go from here.

"Try drawing the gift boxes on the board," Mrs. Ashton suggests, very quietly now. She's standing a little behind me. Blocking me from the rest of the class. "You can draw twenty-five gift boxes, right?"

I grit my teeth, but I start drawing. I take more time than I probably need. I make them look really fancy. One has polka dot wrapping paper. One has flowers on it. Another has skulls.

Five boxes.

Another five.

Another five.

Another five.

And the last five.

I let out a deep breath. There's a square of gift boxes on the board. Five by five. Right. I remember that from multiplication tables.

"Good," Mrs. Ashton says. "Now can you draw me six pieces of ribbon?"

Six pieces of ribbon. To the right of the boxes I draw six long ribbons. I stop again.

"Can you cut each ribbon into ten pieces?" Mrs. Ashton asks.

Okay. I count carefully. I draw cuts into the ribbon until each one is in ten pieces. I realize what she's doing then. "Each piece is one foot," I say.

"Yes, that's right." Mrs. Ashton moves to stand in front of the board. She taps her fingers next to the cut-up ribbons. "Can you stack the pieces of ribbon on top of the stacks of gifts? Each stack needs to have the same amount of ribbon."

I erase the pieces of ribbon one by one and redraw them on top of the presents. Then I stop and look at what I have.

Each stack of five gifts has twelve pieces of ribbon. Mrs. Ashton takes a different color marker, and draws a box around four of the stacks. "You can ignore these," she says. "Focus on the first stack."

Twelve pieces of ribbon and five gifts. I frown at the board. I use my palm to wipe away the twelve pieces of ribbon. I draw them to the left of the five gifts. Then I draw lines connecting them to the gifts.

Two to each. And two left over.

"Good," Mrs. Ashton says. "What you have left is two feet of ribbon that needs to be shared by five gifts." She writes *2 shared among 5* on the board. "Draw another two long ribbons to the left."

I do what she says. She has me cut these into five pieces.

"Each of these ribbons is one-fifth of a foot," she says. "One out of five pieces."

"I get it!" I say. I draw lines under each row of ribbons and gifts. "And there are two of these one-out-of-five pieces."

"Exactly. This is represented by the fraction two-fifths." Next to my lines, she writes *2/5*.

"Okay," I say. "Each gift gets two ribbons. So that makes two-fifths ribbon?"

"Yes," Mrs. Ashton says. "So how much all together?"

"Two," I say, circling the two big pieces of ribbon in the top row. "And two of these fifths. So two and two-fifths."

"Very good, Airi. Each box gets two and two-fifths feet of ribbon." Mrs. Ashton smiles at me. I feel hot all over again, but not like I'm going to explode. I feel the way I do when I pull off a good prank. I don't even mind that it took me twice as long as Wyatt to finish. I did it. I figured out the problem. I've never done that before. And I even understand what I did. I can picture having the gifts in front of me and cutting up pieces of ribbon.

I walk back to my desk feeling like I'm on a cloud. I almost forget that the entire thing was supposed to be a distraction for Mrs. Ashton. Until I sit back down and open my notebook. My mission plan stares up at me. I can't believe I let the enemy get to me like that. She's more cunning than I gave her credit for.

I let my guard down. I won't make that mistake again.

I play it cool the rest of the week. I don't get in any trouble, but I don't play nice either. I keep my head down. It's hard, because I have so many ideas. I keep myself entertained by drawing comics in my notebook. My newest character is a

pirate assassin. I don't have a name for
her yet. Nothing seems cool enough.

It seems to take forever for Friday
to come. By the time it arrives, I'm so
excited that I can't keep still. I hide E.J.'s
books from him. I put Mom's car keys in
the fridge. I take out the laces from Dad's
running shoes. Nothing big. Just enough to keep
me from feeling like I'm about to burst out of my skin.

Before our independent rotations on Friday, Mrs. Ashton
comes to collect our packets. Then she checks them and
hands them back after lunch so she can go over anything
that we got wrong. I open my social studies book and watch
as she goes to her desk, stack of packets in hand.

She opens the first one. Her forehead wrinkles. She flips
through the pages. She sets it aside and opens the next one.
Her frown gets deeper. She flips through this one faster.
Then she starts checking through the pile. I can tell when she
gets to mine, because she stops and looks at it for a while.

Finally she looks up. She sees me watching her. I smile.
After a moment, she starts to smile too. She silently claps
her hands in acknowledgment before writing something on
my sheet. Then she puts it back in the pile and starts looking through everyone's work again.

Once the independent period is over, Mrs. Ashton
returns to the front of the classroom. "I hope you all enjoyed this week's homework," she tells everyone, handing
the packets back to be passed around to their owners. "I

certainly enjoyed looking it over. Good job, everyone."

There are some nervous giggles. Jason already knows it was me, and after I heard Emma asking Liam if she should check with Mrs. Ashton that it wasn't a mistake, I told Mei too. I figured she'd be able to convince people to just play along.

But Mrs. Ashton continues to smile, seeming genuinely amused. Everyone relaxes. The people who have already taken their packet back compare their work. The classroom fills with bubbles of laughter.

Mrs. Ashton's worksheets always have three or four questions with a blank space below for us to answer. But this time, each page is completely blank, except for one sentence written on the first page:

DRAW ANYTHING YOU WANT.

My packet is full of pirate and superhero doodles. That's what's been on my mind lately. On the last page, I drew myself as Luffy[27] from *One Piece* standing with my hands on my hips. The little speech bubble says, *How's this for a prank? I bet you can't do better.*

At the bottom of the page, Mrs. Ashton has written, *Very impressive, Airi. You win this round.*

The glove has been thrown.[28] Let's see Mrs. Ashton *try* to beat this.

---

27 It's pronounced LOO-fee, not LUH-fee. A lot of people get that wrong.

28 This is how people used to challenge people to a duel. They'd throw their glove at someone's face. I don't know why they did that. Maybe because it's annoying to get hit in the face with a glove?

At recess, Jason catches up with me as I'm walking to the cafeteria to buy a snack. I glance at him. "What'd you think?"

Jason grins. "I've never seen anything like that. I thought you were going to put an air horn under her chair or something."

"That's not a bad idea," I say.

A few other people from our class start drifting over, having heard some of our conversation. Liam pokes me in the shoulder and asks, "Was that really you?"

I just smile. His eyes widen, and he runs off to spread the word. Soon everyone knows that I'm the one who freed us from the week's homework. They wave at me when I walk by. Some yell, "Thank you!" It's almost like being a celebrity.

"Aren't you afraid Mrs. Ashton is going to find out?" Jason asks me.

"She already knows," I say. I get my yogurt, and we sit down under a tree so I can fill him in on Mrs. Ashton's challenge and my plans. The more I talk, the bigger his eyes get. After I finish explaining, he sits there quietly while I eat. Apparently it's a lot to take in. I have to admit, it is a pretty impressive plan.

"I want to help," he says eventually.

"Are you sure?" I ask. "We might get in trouble."

"As long as we don't do anything *really* bad," Jason says. "Mrs. Ashton is cool."

I roll my eyes. "No teacher is *cool*. That's the point."

"Come on," Jason says. He elbows me. "You're going to need help. Maybe we can ask Mei."

"Why do you want to, though?" I ask. "You like Mrs. Ashton."

"Sure," Jason says. "That doesn't mean that school isn't *boring*. Ever since you got here, it's been interesting. And this sounds like *loads* of fun."

"Fine," I say. "But remember, traitors face the ultimate punishment." I draw my finger across my neck.

Jason nods seriously. "I know. I still want in."

"We'll have a dangerous fight ahead of us," I tell him. "Our enemy knows we're coming, and she's prepared. But I promise I will take responsibility for any and all consequences, as long as you promise to do as I say."

"I promise to follow your orders to the letter, General Sano." He salutes.

General Sano. I like the sound of it.

Then Jason holds out his hand. "Shake on it?"

I stare at his hand. This feels like a significant moment. I stick my hand in his. We shake. He grins at me.

I think we really are friends now.

PERSONNEL FILE

Name
Hamilton, Jason

Date of Birth
January 31

Place of Birth
San Diego, California

Place of Residence
Fort Shafter, Hawai'i

Occupation
Student

Primary Specialties
Photography, studying

Awards and Citations
Most Surprising Classmate

Disciplinary Record
Probably none

Remarks
While Jason seems eager to join me in my prank competition, he's also mentioned that he thinks Mrs. Ashton is "cool" (which I guess is the reason he says he'll go along with it—she's supposedly the kind of "cool" who won't get mad). It's cute that he thinks that. But no teacher is truly cool. One day Mrs. Ashton will crack, and he'll see. I almost feel bad for him. It's better to be jaded like me. Less disappointment that way.

That being said, I don't think it will hold him back. He's willing and ready to go at my command. And I don't think I'm going to do anything he won't approve of. The point is to make a scene. A dramatic declaration. A demonstration of who I am and what I can accomplish. And it's to challenge Mrs. Ashton to live up to what she claims she is. A "cool" teacher. A champion prankster. I'll believe it when I see it.

19

MRS. ASHTON'S REVENGE COMES QUICKLY.
I don't see it coming. She's smart. Too smart. I have to be more careful. If I'm honest, I didn't really believe she would do anything. That was a mistake.

It happens after lunch. Mrs. Ashton is at the front of the class, ready to begin today's language arts lesson. Then she stops and looks around.

"Oh, shoot," she says. "I let Mrs. Higa borrow my white-board cleaner. Would someone mind getting it for me?"

My hand shoots up in the air. "I'll do it!" I say. A free excuse to leave class? Always.

"Thank you very much, Airi," Mrs. Ashton says. "Her class is right next door, so it shouldn't take you more than a minute."

As if. I can stretch any task out for ages if I want. I've perfected the art of procrastination.

I go to Mrs. Higa's class and stand outside until it sounds like she's come to a pause in her teaching. I peek inside and wave. Mrs. Higa is a teeny-tiny Japanese lady, even tinier than my mom, with dyed brown hair. She seems kind of strict. I'm glad I don't have her.

"Mrs. Ashton sent me to get her whiteboard cleaner back," I say when she nods at me.

Mrs. Higa frowns and taps her chin. Then she shakes her head and says, "Darn, I loaned it to Mr. Ramos."

"Um," I say. "Where is he?"

"Room 102," she says.

So off I go.

Mr. Ramos teaches third grade. His class turns to look at me when I come in. I can tell the kids are impressed by one of the sixth graders being there. We probably seem so big and grown-up to them. I tell Mr. Ramos what I'm there for.

"Oh, I gave it to Miss Kaneshiro," he says.

Does the entire school only have one bottle of cleaner? I grit my teeth and thank him before asking where Miss Kaneshiro is.

This time I get sent to the first-grade classrooms. Miss Kaneshiro looks sad and says she gave the cleaner to Mrs. Evans.

By now I'm annoyed. But it isn't until I get to Mrs. Evans and she tells me that Ms. Kim has it that I figure out what Mrs. Ashton has done. Still, I go to Ms. Kim, then to Mr. Shigura, and finally to Miss Liliana in the office, who says she just sent a student worker to give it back to Mrs. Ashton.

I know better. I haven't seen a single other kid out in the hallways this whole time.

I go back to Mrs. Ashton's classroom. When I get there, she's wiping off the board, cleaning away every streak until it's a pristine white. She gives me a goofy smile.

"Would you believe it, I found the bottle in my desk drawer!" she says. "I'd lose my head if it weren't attached to my neck."

"I see how it is," I say to her.

Mrs. Ashton just gives me a big smile and goes back to cleaning the board. I shuffle back to my seat and flop down. She even managed to ruin skipping class for me. She's good. She's very, very good. I'm going to have to really bring my A game.

AFTER ACTION REPORT

Date
Friday, October 8

Location
Joe Takata Elementary

Actions Undertaken
Opening prank

Duration
One week

Purpose
Beginning the prank war

Mission Result
Complete success

Remarks
A complete success, even counting Mrs. Ashton's little
prank later. I pulled it off perfectly. Neither Mrs. Ashton
nor Ms. Nicole knew anything was wrong until today.
And no one told them. That kind of surprised me. Out of
twenty-five kids, you'd think one might be a tattletale or
just be clueless enough to ask the teacher if they made a
mistake and spoil all the fun. But I guess even kids who
like school are excited to get out of doing work and do
something fun instead.

OVER THE WEEKEND, DAD TAKES US ALL TO THE BEACH.
Preparing for the beach is like packing for an expedition. Mom and Dad have to make sure they have everything Kaori needs, including little cooling patches for her head if it gets too hot. We pack a big cooler of food and water. We bring lots of sunscreen and bamboo mats to lie on. And of course we bring everything we need for the ocean: towels, snorkels, goggles, boogie boards.

Since we're taking Kaori, we go to Ala Moana. It's got a nice calm beach. All the waves are way out there. You can walk far out into the water, which is perfectly clear, and you'll still be able to just stand there without getting hit in the face with a wave, like at Waikīkī. What's fun is that after you walk out far enough, the sand suddenly drops away and the water turns a dark blue. I like to dance along the edge, feeling the sand slip beneath my feet.

Dad takes me out to paddle around on the boogie board. I can tell he's trying to make me feel better after the fight last week. And I don't want to be mad at him. Even though I can't stop thinking about how he might leave soon. Every time I remember, I get a little mad again. I just want to have fun with him. I let him show me some tricks for when Cousin Layla finally teaches me to surf. Dad used to be really good at surfing, but he's out of practice now.

Mom only goes a little way into the water. She doesn't like to swim much. After she dips her toes in, she retreats to the shade. She's had less energy lately. Even when it comes to scolding me. Kaori loves the water. She looks so cute with her big inflatable arm floaties. Her swim cap has tiny fish on it. I refuse to wear a swim cap anymore. It makes my head too hot. Mom always wants me to because if I don't, my hair is *huge* after it dries.

E.J. is practicing his breaststroke a little bit away from me. He has to wear special goggles in the water so he can see. They make him look like a big frog. I dive underneath the water and mermaid my way to him. I wait until the perfect moment, then push myself up as fast as I can and grab his ankles.

E.J. screams. I surface, grinning, as he frantically flails his arms. When he sees me, he groans and splashes water in my face. The salt stings my eyes.

HOW TO MERMAID . . .

How to mermaid: Take a deep breath and then dive down as deep as you can, preferably to the bottom. Make a wave with your body to move forward. It's great for stealth attacks.

"Ouch," I say.

"You suck, Airi," he says. "Are you trying to drown me?"

"I'm just trying to keep you on your toes," I say. "What if I were a shark?"

"Sharks don't come this far in," E.J. says.

"That's what they thought in *Jaws*," I say. I lunge as if to bite him, and he shrieks.

"Ugh, you're so *weird*!" he says. He kicks me in the leg and swims off as fast as he can. He's a really good swimmer.

I swim back to shore, keeping my body in the water as long as possible, until I'm pressed fully against the sand with my head poking out. Mom and Kaori are standing at the edge of the water, letting the water lap over their feet. Kaori is giggling and splashing her feet. Even Mom is smiling, one of her real beautiful smiles. Mom has a great smile. I wish she did it more.

Suddenly I'm sick of the ocean. I get out and go to our mats to dry off. I pull an Otter Pop from our cooler—strawberry flavor—and eat it so fast I get brain freeze. The juice gets all over my hand and dries sticky. I stick my fingers in my mouth. Mom isn't here to tell me not to.

At home, I check out my tan. It's just a little visible, but I don't look so pale. Now Noah can't tease me for looking whiter than him. I drag my hair over my face. It's all big and a little stiff with salt.

I go downstairs. E.J. is at the dining table working on something. I look over his shoulder. "Is that a test?"

He pokes his elbow back, trying to get me in the ribs. I know him, though. "It's a placement test," he says. "My teacher thinks I would do better with more of a challenge." He turns around and gives me a smile. "I get to skip a grade, up to yours."

"If that happens," I say, "I'll quit school forever and run away to live in the mountains."

E.J. snorts. "Dad would track you down."

"He won't even be here," I say. "So he won't."

E.J. looks down. "Do you think he's really going to leave?"

I don't know. I don't want him to. But I know better than to let myself think he'll stay. It's happened before. When we were living in Kentucky, he was supposed to be home. Then he suddenly got sent to Europe. He was gone for ages. Mom was pregnant with Kaori and was too tired to do much. E.J.

and I spent a lot of time at the neighbors' houses. We didn't even get to see Dad on video calls, because his assignment was classified.

E.J. actually sounds like he'll miss Dad. Which is way different from the other day. Maybe he was just pretending not to care. That would be like him.

"He always leaves," I say. I pick up one of E.J.'s spare pencils and draw a big smiley face on his paper before he can push me away.

I pass Mom on my way back upstairs. She's leaning against the wall and braiding her hair. I walk past her, then turn around and go, "RAH!"

Mom doesn't even flinch. She just says, "Not now, Airi."

Not that it ever is *now*. Mom never seems to want me around. I suddenly don't want to see anyone for the rest of the weekend. I announce, "I'm going to hibernate," and go back to my room. I pull the bedsheets around the lower bunk so I'm in a little cave.

I curl up in the farthest corner of the bed and stare at the glow-in-the-dark star stickers I put up on the underside of the top bunk. I made up a bunch of constellations for it, even though I know the real ones. Dad taught them to me, and the stories that go with them. Makali'i the navigator and his net full of fish. Iwikuamoʻo, the backbone of the sky. Hoku-lei, the wreath of stars. Dad says people see what they're familiar with in the stars. My constellations are things like Mr. Knuckles. The swirl of Kaori's hair. A tree from Grandma and Grandpa's farm. Sailors used to use constellations to find their way home. I think that's pretty cool. When I was really little, I wanted to be an astronaut. Then I found out how much math and science they have to know. I'll wait until we have hotels on Mars. I won't have to learn anything for that.

When Dad taught the stars to me, I was really young and sad that he was about to leave. He showed me the different patterns and told me that where he was going would have the same stars overhead. So I should look at them and know that he was looking at them too.

I know now that's not how time differences work. He was just trying to make me feel better. That's what grown-ups do. They tell you things to make you feel better, even if they aren't true. That's why you can't trust them.

SITUATION REPORT

Date
Monday, October 11

Location
Joe Takata Elementary

Activities Planned
Organizing my prank squad

Logistical Requirements
None

Obstacles Anticipated
I trust Jason to find good recruits, but there's always a chance one of them is a spy or a tattletale.

Remarks
I recruited Mei for the prank squad on the bus to school. She rolled her eyes and said it sounded silly. Then she asked when we were meeting. So she's in.

I've never had a team before. It feels a little like we're a gang of thieves or spies. And they have to listen to what I say! Because that's what they're agreeing to! I could get used to that.

JASON BRINGS ME THREE RECRUITS FOR OUR FIRST mission. Emma Kapono, Wyatt Hirai, and Liam Hunt. Everyone except Liam lives on base—that's why Jason knows them well enough to ask. And Liam is Wyatt's best friend. They go everywhere together.

My new squad. We gather during recess to discuss our strategy.

"Shape up, recruits," I tell them. "You're going to need nerves of steel and absolute determination. Do you have what it takes?"

Mei snaps to attention and salutes. You can tell her dad is a soldier too. "Yes, sir!"

The others copy her. They aren't as military regimented as Mei, but they do okay. Even Liam. I pace in front of them, hands behind my back. They look ready. But I'll still have to test them.

Name: Wyatt Hirai
Expertise: Better than twenty-twenty vision and the fastest runner in the grade

Name: Emma Kapono
Expertise: Hawaiian history and violin

Name: Liam Hunt
Expertise: Skateboarding and *Fortnite*

"Here's an easy one to start, just to get us all warmed up," I say. "Over the next day or two, any time Mrs. Ashton asks for someone to come to the board, you are going to volunteer. When you leave, you'll take the marker you were using with you and hide it in your backpack. Do you think you can do that?"

"Yes, sir!" they all say.

"Then you have your orders," I say. "Dismissed!"

Mei and Jason stay behind. "Permission to speak?" Mei asks. She's standing perfectly straight.

"At ease," I tell her. She relaxes.

"What if Mrs. Ashton borrows markers from other teachers?" she asks.

"Then we'll keep taking them," I say.

"And then what?"

"That's a secret," I say. I don't actually have a plan yet. But I will soon. I've been thinking about it *constantly.* I lie awake at night and imagine how different pranks might go. I've never been this excited to come to school. I'll show Mrs. Ashton who's the real prankmaster.

By lunch the next day, Mrs. Ashton is down to one marker. She knows that we took them. I can tell from how she stops calling on my accomplices to come to the board. That's okay. I've got the next step ready.

It came to me while I was watching TV with E.J. It's pretty genius, if I do say so myself.

At lunch I collect all the markers. Then I put them in a takeout container from the cupboard at home. Behind the

school office building is a bunch of bird-of-paradise plants. I send Jason with the box to bury it as best he can in the dirt. Then I show them what I've drawn.

It's a treasure map of the school. I have our classroom, Fort Ashton. The hallways are ocean ways. I've written *HERE THERE BE DRAGONS* over the parking lot. The office is Skeleton Island. X marks the spot. I even stained the paper with Dad's coffee to make it look old.

I had Mei put a piece of tape over the door to Mrs. Ashton's classroom so it wouldn't lock. So I can sneak in and write on the board, *WE HAVE YOUR MARKERS. TRY TO FIND THEM.* I draw a skull and crossbones underneath. Then I set the map on her desk.

I take the tape off when I leave. Leave no trace behind. That's key to a good prank. The last marker goes into my backpack.

I'm expecting frustration. Anger. At the very least, annoyance. Whiteboard markers are the most important things a teacher has. Without them, they're powerless.

Instead, when Mrs. Ashton sees our ransom note, she says, "This will be fun," and shows everyone the treasure map. Then she asks all of us to help her figure out where the markers are hidden. And I can't just not say anything. That would be too suspicious. But I also can't tell her where they are or be too obvious about trying to trick her.

Everyone has ideas. There's an argument about whether Skeleton Island is the gym or the playground. They get distracted by the dragon I drew in the corner. Then Malia says something about the birds-of-paradise.

"See?" she says, pointing at Skeleton Island. "There are birds flying around the X."

I should have made the map harder to read. But it had to make sense. I have to be fair.

Mrs. Ashton leads us all on an expedition to unearth the markers. The whole class begins digging around the flowers. I hope Jason buried the container deep.

My five pranksters blend in. I have to say that I'm proud of them. All of them are doing a good job of playing innocent. Even I almost believe they had nothing to do with this.

Chloe yells. "Found it!" she cries. She emerges from the plants. Her face is smudged with dirt. In her hands she's clutching the box of markers.

Mrs. Ashton accepts the box like it's the most precious treasure on earth. "Wonderful. Thank you, everyone, for your help." She smiles at all of us, but especially me. I resist the urge to stick out my tongue.

Back in the classroom, Mrs. Ashton dusts off the markers and puts them back on their tray. Then she picks up teaching like nothing happened. Now *I'm* annoyed. Is this how Mrs. Ashton is going to fight this prank war? Just pretend that it isn't happening? Seems like she was lying about being the best prankster. She hasn't even done anything yet except for the whiteboard-cleaner thing, and that was so low-effort it hardly counts. She didn't have to do anything except ask some teachers to play along.

This was supposed to be fun, but now it just feels kind of pointless. Maybe I should disband my crew. I look down at my notebook, where I've written my plans and ideas. Still . . . if she isn't going to retaliate, maybe this war will be easier to win than I thought. Which I guess would prove that she's all talk. But it doesn't feel satisfying to win because the other side never even tried.

During math the next day, I get up to sharpen my pencil. I could get a small sharpener to keep at my desk, but I like the WHIRRR sound the electric one makes. We're doing some "individual practice," which means we do worksheets while Mrs. Ashton and Ms. Nicole walk around and answer questions. As I'm coming back to my desk, I glance at Mei's paper. The first thing I notice is how neat her handwriting is. Then I see that her sheet looks a little different from mine.

I wait until we're on the bus to ask her if I can see her worksheet. "I want to check my answers," I tell her.

"You're not allowed to copy off me," she says, pulling her backpack up to her lap. She takes out her math folder and hands me the sheet. "I'm watching you."

I look at Mei's worksheet. I don't care about her answers. What I care about are the questions. Because now that I'm looking at Mei's sheet, I realize that mine has some extra things added to it. A key to fractions and math symbols, and definitions of some words. My word problems are written different from hers too. Mine use easier words.

Anger and embarrassment rise in me. I've actually kind of been enjoying math ever since Mrs. Ashton showed me

the drawing trick. I can turn most questions into games. But now it turns out she's babying me? I'm not stupid. I don't need special treatment. Did she think I wouldn't find out?

"Thanks," I tell Mei, handing the sheet back. Now there's no way I'm going to continue playing the good student. I take out my own worksheet and my big eraser and start rubbing out all my work.

"What are you doing?" Mei asks, sounding alarmed.

"Don't worry about it," I tell her.

I turn in the worksheet completely blank. It's a protest. It's a demonstration. That you can't fix me with one little math trick and by giving me easier work. I'm still a trouble-maker. I'm still a bad student. I'm craving the familiar sight of the big red F at the top of my sheet. A badge to remind me of who I really am.

But when Mrs. Ashton returns the graded worksheets, she has folded mine into a butterfly. She has even drawn patterns on the wings. She doesn't say anything about me not doing the work. She doesn't even give me a note for my parents.

I want to ask her why. But at the same time, I don't want her to think I care why. I shouldn't. I should just care that I'm getting away with not doing work. The old me would have been thrilled. But I'm not. I feel weird. Kind of empty. I shove the butterfly into my backpack.

For our weekend assignment, Mrs. Ashton asks us to write a paragraph about the book we're reading at home. I write, *I'm not reading anything*, and then draw a dinosaur. When I get that paper back, I see that Mrs. Ashton has added a city beneath the dinosaur's feet. There are little people running from it. She gave the dinosaur a word bubble too.

STOP! it says. *YOU FORGOT YOUR KEYS!*

I scowl and shove it into my backpack. But at home I take it out again. I can't think why Mrs. Ashton would do this. No other teacher has ever played along like this. The last time I turned in a drawing instead of an assignment, Mrs. Robertson called my mom in for a meeting (Dad was traveling for work) to discuss my "persistent disregard for education." I don't understand why Mrs. Ashton hasn't done the same thing yet.

What I especially hate is that I think I'm starting to like Mrs. Ashton. Even though she gave me an easier worksheet without telling me. Even though she told my parents about my reading. Because she's funny. And the way she teaches is fun. Interesting. She answers any question people have, even if it seems kind of silly. Like the other day, Liam asked her what "booty" is. He thought it meant "butt." The whole class laughed at him. Even me. But Mrs. Ashton answered him.

"It's true, it has come to mean that in modern slang," Mrs. Ashton said, smiling. "The original meaning was referring to stolen goods, usually taken after a battle."

Which I already knew because of pirates. I thought it was something everyone knew. If he'd asked me, I'd have laughed at him and made fun of him. But Mrs. Ashton took him seriously. She does that for everything. I'm not used to it.

I don't want to like Mrs. Ashton. Because eventually she'll stop liking me. Like how Mom used to find me funny and now gets annoyed. Or how E.J. used to play with me. Or how every teacher I've had who started out being friendly and nice ended up hating me. So I can't be her friend. I have to keep fighting her.

I take out my social studies homework: a blank map we're supposed to label with the different parts of the Roman Empire. I write, *I'm not going to do work no matter what you do.*

I let myself get too comfortable. I forgot that Mrs. Ashton isn't a friend. She's still a teacher. And I'm not going to do what she wants.

INCIDENT REPORT

Date
Tuesday, October 19

Location
Joe Takata Elementary

Event Description
Once again, Mrs. Ashton didn't punish me for not doing my work. Instead she added flowers around the edge of the map and wrote, *I don't give up.*

It's weird. I guess this is kind of what I wanted. I don't have to do work. But not because the teacher doesn't care. She's letting me turn in blank papers. And she isn't telling my parents, because if she had, I would have had a talk with Mom, at the very least. It feels like I'm getting away with something but also like I'm playing her game. Whatever that game is. I don't like not knowing where I stand or what's coming next. I can't predict her at all.

ON WEDNESDAY, I GET HOME AND DiG AROUND iN MY backpack for my lunch bag so I can put it out for the next day. Except that it isn't in there.

What *is* in there is a pencil box with Sailor Moon on it. A girly-looking book that I saw Mei reading last week. A butterfly clip. A notebook full of Mei's neat, perfect writing.

"What?" I say.

A few minutes later, the phone rings. I pick up and say, "Yellow?"

"Airi? Is that you?" It's Emma. "I think I have your school supplies. Your lunch bag is in my backpack."

I look at my backpack. It's definitely my backpack, but the stuff inside isn't mine. "I think I have Mei's stuff," I tell her. "Do you have her phone number?"

When Mei answers the phone, she says she thinks she

has Liam's stuff. And Liam says he has Wyatt's, and Wyatt says he has Jason's. By then I'm pretty sure I know whose stuff Jason has, but I call him anyway. Sure enough, he has Emma's things.

"Should we all meet to exchange?" Jason asks. Most of our crew lives on the base, and Liam lives right nearby, though they're all on the other side of it from where Mei and me live.

I groan. "Okay," I say.

I meet up with Mei, and we bike over to meet the others by the bowling lanes. We make the exchange in the parking lot. I dig out Mei's school supplies and hand them over. I'm about to put my own stuff back in my bag when I notice a fluorescent Post-it note at the bottom.

I pull it out, already feeling a sense of dread. I'm pretty sure I know who's behind this. Sure enough, on the Post-it is Mrs. Ashton's writing: *Gotcha!*

"Soldiers," I say grimly, "we've been pranked." I show them all the note. "That means she's figured us out."

Jason hangs his head. "We failed in being stealthy, then."

"Or Mrs. Ashton is just smart," I point out. "I wasn't expecting her to catch on so fast. I understand if you want to back out now."

Mei scoffs. "As if." She tosses her hair and hitches up her backpack. "I'm going to get Kiana and Grace to help. The more people we have, the better. Then she can't pick out the culprits as fast."

I'm impressed. Mei is made of stronger stuff than she

looks. "Well," I say, "in that case, pass this around."

I pull out the sheet of paper I've been writing on for the past few days. I have twenty key words on there. Our cues.

"You'll need to fill your water bottles with soda," I say. "Unless you can burp on command." I demonstrate.

"Ew," Mei and Liam say in unison.

Emma swallows and then lets out a magnificent *BRAAAAAAP*. "Like that?" she asks.

"Exactly," I say to her. "Do you want to practice?"

We sit around and practice burping, even though Mei says it's gross, until a bunch of old men come up and make us move so they can go bowling. I burp "Aloha" at them. They give us all the stink eye.

"You're real lolo, you know that?" Emma says to me. "But pretty cool."

"Thank you," I say. We high-five.

"See you," Wyatt says to us, hopping back on his skateboard. "I gotta get back home before Mom sends the base cops after me."

We all say goodbye. Jason gives me a smile and a thumbs-up before he goes. Mei is leaning on her bike. It's pink and has a white basket in front. She hops onto the seat. She's smart. Even though she wears skirts every day, she always has shorts on underneath.

"Why are you doing this?" I ask her. "I thought you were all goody-goody."

Mei raises her eyebrow at me. She's better at it than I am. "Yeah. But this is sixth grade." She tightens her ponytail.

"It's our last chance to act like kids before it all becomes really serious. That's what my mom says. After this we'll be in middle school, and things will be different."

I get on my bike too. "Different how?"

"Like, we have to start thinking about *college*." Mei shakes her head. "And people start dating in middle school. I can't mess that up."

"Ew," I say. "We're *eleven*. Who wants to date? There are so many better things to do."

"You can't go alone to school dances," Mei says. She kicks off and starts biking away. I have to pedal quickly to catch up with her. "Only losers do that."

"That's so—" I don't know what to say.

"Don't worry," Mei calls. "I'll make sure you aren't a loser. You might be weird, but you're my friend now. And I don't ever let my friends down."

My chest feels funny. Like it's full of fireworks. Mei bikes away, flashing me a peace sign over her shoulder. She looks so cool with her hair flying behind her.

I bike home, excited to tell Mom and Dad that I definitely for real made a friend—she even said so. I'm pretty sure Jason is my friend too, but he hasn't said it for sure. And Mei is different, because she didn't like me at first. I changed her mind. That's pretty cool.

I drag my bike into the

garage and kick off my shoes at the door before going inside. Everyone is in the kitchen, even Kaori. She's in her high chair with a bunch of Cheerios. I pretend to steal her nose and wiggle my thumb at her. She shrieks with laughter and tries to grab my hand.

Mom, Dad, and E.J. are looking at some piece of paper. I crowd in behind them and ask, "What are we looking at?"

"E.J.'s placement test results," Dad says. "He did well enough to get into a few pretty good private schools."

"Oh," I say. Of course. E.J. is a little genius. "That's cool, I guess."

"What about the cost?" Mom asks Dad. "Maybe I should start working again."

"What about the kids?" Dad asks. "They'll need someone at home."

"There is the daycare for Kaori," Mom says. "Airi and E.J. will have to do after-school programs until I pick them up."

"It isn't a bad idea, but what about when I'm overseas?" My stomach drops. He's talking about it like it's a sure thing. He hasn't talked about it since the fight. I'd hoped that meant he was going to say no. But it doesn't sound like that.

Mom presses her lips together and looks back at me and E.J. "Please take Kaori for her nap. Dad and I need to talk."

"You mean argue," I say. Mom and Dad don't argue very much. Neither of them like doing it. When they do, they always make us leave.

"No, we're not going to argue," Dad says. "We just need to have a grown-up talk."

"That's just grown-up code for 'argument,'" I say. I go and lift Kaori out of her high chair. "Come on, E.J."

E.J. waits until we're upstairs to ask, "Do you really think they're arguing?"

I roll my eyes as I kick open the door to Kaori's room. "Duh. If you go to private school, it's gonna cost money. You'll have to get a scholarship. You had to be all fancy, didn't you?"

"I didn't mean to." E.J. hovers in the doorway to Kaori's room. "The teacher just said that it would be more challenging."

"You didn't have to *listen*." I wrap Kaori up in her blanket the way Mom taught me and walk around the room bouncing her up and down until she starts to get sleepy. "You always have to be special. Now Mom and Dad are fighting. Dad's definitely gonna leave now."

"No," E.J. says. His voice sounds weird. I look over. His eyes are all blurry. "Don't say that. Shut up."

"You shut up," I say. "Can't you just be normal?"

"Like you?" E.J. snaps. "You can't even read!"

I go very cold. But not like I'm scared.

I'm mad.

I'm furious, actually. Because that means E.J. listened in on me and our parents. Or they told him. Which would be way worse. But either way, I can't stand him knowing. And I can't stand him using it against me.

I carefully put Kaori down in her crib. She doesn't need be here for this. I push E.J. out of her room and shove him into the wall. "You're a slimy little suck-up," I tell him, as nastily as I can. "If you weren't trying to show off all the time, they wouldn't have to worry about money. Dad for sure can't tell them he doesn't want to go to Guam now. He has to work extra hard and do everything they say because of *you*."

E.J. starts crying. "I hate you!" he shouts. He turns and runs down the hall.

"I hate you too!" I scream back.

Inside her room, Kaori starts crying. I start to stomp back up to my room. Just let her cry. She'll calm down soon.

Then I deflate. I don't know why I said those things to E.J. I don't know why I feel like this all the time. I never liked being mean before we moved here. I think there's something wrong with me.

I go into Kaori's room and pick her up again. "Shh," I say to her. I rock her. "Everything is going to be okay."

Eventually she settles down again. Mom and Dad's "grown-up talk" is over. I can tell because I can smell food. I think Dad is cooking tonight, because it smells like Spam. I go downstairs. Dad is standing at the stove with an apron on. He's frying Spam in a pan. There's a bowl of day-old rice next to him.

I wrap my arms around his waist and press my face into his back. Dad startles. Then he pats my hand.

"Do you want to help me out?" he asks.

"No," I say into his back. "I need to do something nice for E.J."

"Hmm." Dad continues to stir the Spam. "He likes red

bean pastry. How about that? Shouldn't take you too long. I'll walk you through it if you forgot how."

It's really easy to make manjū the way Grandma Sano does. You only need a few ingredients: flour, sugar, salt, vegetable oil, some cold water, and a can of sweet red bean paste. We bake ours, because it makes them all flaky and delicious, but you can steam them too.

Dad turns on the oven for me. I tuck a dish towel into my collar—the flour gets *everywhere*—and follow his instructions. The dough is really oily and kind of gross. But I know it comes out better that way. I scoop a little spoon of red bean paste into each disc of dough. Soon I have a tray of lumpy little red bean balls.

They smell good when they're baking. So good that Mom comes by to see what's going on. She's surprised to see that it's me who's making them and has to check on them herself. She doesn't find anything wrong. Of course not. I made them perfectly.

"They're for E.J.," I tell her.

Mom's face softens, and she smiles. "That's very sweet of you, Airi."

I decide not to tell her that they're apology pastries.

After they're done baking and have cooled, I make a little plate of them and take it up to E.J.'s room. His door is

shut tight. He doesn't answer at my knock, so I leave the plate outside. I look down at my front at the flour on the dish towel and drag my finger through it. I write *Sorry* on his door. Then I go back downstairs to put the rest away.

INCIDENT REPORT

Date
Thursday, October 21

Location
Fort Shafter, Hawai'i

Event Description
E.J. and I aren't talking. He isn't making a big deal out of it, but he didn't say anything to me while we waited for the bus. But he ate the manjū. Maybe that's why he didn't tell on me to Mom and Dad.

O N THURSDAY, MEi iS LATE FOR THE BUS FOR THE first time ever. She throws herself into the seat next to me. "A mongoose got in the house," she says. She sounds horrified and thrilled. "They're *so gross*."

"I saw one tear apart a chicken once," I tell her. "I want one as a pet. It would be a great guard animal."

"I definitely wouldn't mess with anyone who had a pet mongoose," Mei says. She pulls out her phone and opens up her text messages. It's so annoying that my parents still say I'm not old enough to have my own phone. I've seen second graders who have one. "I told Grace and Kiana the plan." She shows me. "They're in."

"Excellent." I have a full troop at my disposal. I feel powerful. Like I can do anything. "Tell them to be ready. It starts today."

My new minions gather in front of the school. In addition to Grace and Kiana, Wyatt has recruited his and Liam's friend Joey, and Emma has gotten Whitney. Mei came prepared. She has three cans of Sprite in her backpack that she distributes to us. We all fill our water bottles and crush the cans to better hide the evidence.

Name: Grace Wong
Expertise: Swimming and gymnastics

Name: Kiana Flores
Expertise: Fastest reader in class and speaks three languages (English, Spanish, Mandarin)

Name: Joey Nguyen
Expertise: Tallest kid in the grade and their mom is on the school board

Name: Whitney Lee
Expertise: Piano and basketball

I raise my water bottle. "Cheers, my fellows," I say. "Let's do this."

We clink our water bottles together. Then we march off to the classroom, ready for the next fight.

I made the list of cue words very carefully. I've been keeping track of words Mrs. Ashton uses a lot. But not ones like "the," because that would be too hard to do. Words like "module" and "bias."

She starts class out using one right away. "We're moving on to our Ancient Greece module," she says.

My minions and I all quickly take a sip. Then, like a horrible chorus of frogs: *BRAAAAAAAAAAAAAAAAAAPPPPPPP PPPPPPPPP.*

The class goes silent. All of us look innocently at Mrs. Ashton.

Throughout the day, we keep up the assault.

"Another example—"

BRAAAAP.

"Let's take a moment to review."

BRAAAAPPP.

"In context—"

BRAAAAAAAAAAAAAAAPPPP.

"The best strategy—"

BRAAAAAAAAAAAAAAAAAAPPPPPPPPPPPPPPPPPPP.

By the time we leave for PE, Ms. Nicole looks like she's about to catch fire. Even Mrs. Ashton is starting to look annoyed.

The conspirators gather around on the blacktop and exchange high fives. "It's going great," I tell them. "We have successfully made a hostile environment for learning."

She's standing next to me like she's my second-incommand. Maybe I should make badges. Though she and

Jason would have to be equal rank, since Jason was the first to join me. And I have to honor that.

"Good idea," I say to her. "Okay, good job." I stick my hand into the middle of our circle. "Let's go, team."

We all put our hands in and cheer.

Word of the prank war is spreading through class. Even though we're supposed to be playing four square today, people keep coming over to ask me if it's true and if they can join. I'm going to have to hold tryouts. I can't just let anyone join. You never know who might be a spy for the enemy. So I just shrug and say I'll think about it.

We go back to class and settle into our seats, ready to resume battle. I keep my hand on my water bottle like a cowboy with his pistol. You gotta be fast on the draw.

Mrs. Ashton goes almost ten whole minutes without saying one of the trigger words. I start to wonder if she somehow found the list and is deliberately avoiding them. Then she turns to the board and says, "I'll demonstrate—"

All of us lift our bottles. We take a sip, ready to let loose.

"Blech!" I spit out my mouthful. All around me, my supporters are coughing and making disgusted faces. I can tell that it's still Sprite in the bottle, but there's something wrong with it. It's sour. And bad. I take a hesitant sniff.

Vinegar.

Mrs. Ashton looks around at us. "Is there a problem?" she asks. She smiles.

I turn in that day's work with *ROUND TWO: YOU WIN.*

AFTER ACTION REPORT

Date
Thursday, October 21

Location
Joe Takata Elementary

Actions Undertaken
Burping challenge

Duration
One day

Purpose
Disrupting class

Mission Result
Mixed success

Remarks
We were doing pretty good. It was a good idea, and
my minions did everything right. A lesser enemy would
have sent us out of the room or punished the whole
class if they couldn't figure out who was to blame. But
Mrs. Ashton was smart about it. She got us to punish
ourselves. That's good. So maybe she isn't all talk.
Maybe there really is a prankster underneath all that
teacher-ness. More to come.

24

"**CLEARLY WE NEED TO RETHiNK OuR STRATEGY**," I say to Jason when I see him at lunch. "We aren't going big enough. We have to think of what will have maximum impact."

"I agree," Jason says. "I can still taste the vinegar." He makes a face and scrubs at his tongue with a napkin. "Gross."

"I didn't want to recruit more people so soon," I say, "but to do this right, we need as many people as possible. We need to turn the entire room into a prank gauntlet."

"I have an idea for that," Jason says. Then he tells me what the school does for Halloween. I feel myself lighting up like the Fourth of July. Because it feels like fate. It's the perfect opportunity.

Every classroom gets a small amount of money for the students to decorate it. Last year Jason's class made theirs look like a haunted forest. Everyone brings in candy or other treats. Then everyone goes trick-or-treating through the whole school. Even families can come. *And* the school votes on the best decorated room, and that class gets a pizza party.

"We have to win," I say.

Jason nods seriously. "And Halloween is perfect for pranks."

We look at each other and grin. I'm thinking of all the times I've spooked E.J. by making him think the house was haunted, or the time I dressed in a white shirt covered in ketchup and lay on the floor of my old school's bathroom and pretended to be dead. Jason's right. Halloween *is* perfect for pranks. It might even be better than April Fools' Day, because people aren't trying to compete for it.

I pull out my notebook. "We have about a week until Halloween," I say. I was already looking forward to Halloween. Now I can't wait. I bet I can even figure out a way to use my awesome costume to its full effect. "Between now and then, we need to test everyone. See if they're worthy of joining our cause." I start to draw some haunted house ideas. "We have to give them a test. A Dare Challenge."

Jason asks, "Even me?"

"No," I say. "Original members don't have to. Unless you want to." I already have some ideas for what the test will be. "Spread the word. We'll start tomorrow."

Jason salutes. I could get used to that.

At home I find a sheet of blank mailing labels that

Dad uses for Christmas cards. I label them. Colonel Jason Hamilton. Colonel Mei Ishida. Majors Emma Kapono, Wyatt Hirai, and Liam Hunt. Privates Joey Nguyen and Whitney Lee. Captains Grace Wong and Kiana Flores. And, of course, General Airi Sano.

I'll accept as many people as I have labels for. That's gonna be the rule. If I make it an elite team, it'll seem more impressive. Everyone will try harder. I draw stars and stripes on the labels to match Dad's medals. Then I put the sheet in my backpack for later.

Mom is making udon for dinner, which means she isn't feeling great. I try to make her laugh by turning the stove off and saying the Menehune did it. She shoos me away. So I pick up Kaori and start making her dance on the kitchen counter.

"Look, Mom," I say. I have Kaori strike a disco pose. "Look at that funk and soul."

"That's nice," Mom says without looking up. She goes to open the refrigerator and accidentally knocks a glass bottle of oyster sauce to the floor. Kaori and I wrinkle our noses. Oyster sauce might taste delicious, but it smells really gross.

Mom sighs. "Airi, could you get the broom for me? Be careful with the glass."

I put Kaori back in her seat and go out to the garage for the broom and dustpan. When I get back inside, Mom is wiping up the sauce with a paper towel. I reach behind her and switch the stove off again.

"Airi!" Mom says when she notices.

"Wasn't me," I say. I start sweeping up the glass. "It was the Menehune, I told you. One just ran by. Didn't you see?"

Mom just shakes her head.

So after I throw out the glass, I grab one of my paints and color my fingers green. I walk them across the counter when Mom is chopping green onions and switch the stove off again. Then I quickly wash my hand.

Mom turns and scowls when she sees the flame is out again. I point at the little prints and say, "See? The Menehune were here. They even left footprints this time."

Mom closes her eyes. "Airi, please go to your room."

"Oh, come on," I say. "It's just a joke." I reach for the paper towels to wipe the paint away—I'll be in so much trouble if I don't—and accidentally jostle the pot on the stove. I barely have time to jump back before it topples to the floor, spilling broth and vegetables everywhere. Some splashes on my foot. It's *really* hot.

"Oh crap," I say.

Mom has broth down her front, and there's a piece of carrot that went flying in her hair. She stares at the mess on the floor. For a moment I think she's going to yell at me. But then she covers her face with her hands and starts crying.

I freeze. I don't know what to do. She's sinking into a crouch, still hiding her face. "Mom?" I say. She doesn't look up.

"What was that?" E.J. calls. He comes into the kitchen. He looks around. Sees the mess. Sees me. Sees Mom crying. Sees Kaori watching all of it with big eyes. E.J. looks at me like I'm the worst person in the world. I feel like it too.

"I'll take Kaori upstairs and order us pizza," I say. I can't stay in the kitchen. I feel like I'm going to throw up and also like I'm completely hollow inside. I scoop Kaori up and carry her to her room. Then I go to my room for the phone and call the pizza place. I even order Mom and E.J.'s favorite, Portuguese sausage and onion. I dig out my stash of birthday money and wait at the door for the delivery.

When Dad gets home, the kitchen is clean and we're eating pizza in silence. I'm sitting at the far end of the table from Mom and E.J. He made her a cup of tea, and she isn't crying anymore. Her eyes are still red, though. I can't look at her for too long.

"I'm going to bed," I announce as soon as I've eaten my second slice. I stop to give Dad a quick hug. I hope he doesn't hate me after Mom tells him what happened.

I lie in bed for a while, staring at the ceiling and listening to my iPod. I have a playlist that's all Japanese rock. It's kind of nice, because I don't understand any of the words. I can just listen. I have some others too. I have a K-pop playlist for when I'm doing chores, because it sounds happy. And I have a Japanese metal playlist for when I'm really mad or upset. Sometimes you just need to listen to people scream in a different language and stare at nothing.

Even though I lie there for a long time and count over

one hundred sheep, I don't get tired. It's too early. I give up and creep down the hallway to Kaori's room. I like sitting with her when she's sleeping. She's so peaceful.

I sit there for a while before I hear Mom and Dad come upstairs for bed. They're coming toward Kaori's room, so I quickly hide behind the rocking chair. I wrap my arms around my knees and curl up as small as I can.

"I can't do this," Mom is saying when they come in. "I'm overwhelmed. I thought maybe Airi would help out more, but everything is the same. She's out of control."

"I know." Dad sighs. "I keep hoping it's a phase, but she hasn't gotten any better, has she? Her teacher is optimistic, but she says Airi still isn't engaging in class."

My entire body goes cold and shaky at Dad's words. I hate it when Dad's disappointed in me. And I feel the same swoop of hurt at what Mrs. Ashton said. Which is silly, because I shouldn't care if she likes me. But maybe I do. I curl up even tighter. As far into the corner as I can get.

"I can't handle her and everything else as it is," Mom says. "I need you home."

"I don't have a choice, Reiko," Dad says. He sounds sad. "If they offer me the assignment, I have to take it. That's been made clear to me."

"What if you didn't? What would happen?"

"It's necessary if I want to be promoted—"

"What does that matter?"

"It's the pension, you know that. We have three kids. They're going to go to college someday."

Now Mom sounds like she's crying again. "I wish you weren't in the military. I wish I'd made you leave sooner."

"Reiko—" Dad switches into Japanese, the way he does when Mom gets really upset. It's too quiet to really hear, but I catch a few words every now and then. Enough to know that he's saying sorry and trying to cheer her up.

Eventually, they leave, after saying good night to Kaori. I wait a while longer before standing up. Kaori is sleeping soundly. It must be nice to be a baby. You don't have to be sorry about anything. Or feel guilty. Or be sad.

I lean in and kiss her on the forehead. "Good night, Kaori," I say. "You're the lucky one in this house."

She sleeps on, completely unaware.

I go back to my room and hide in my bunk bed with a sketchbook. If you ever mention you like to draw, all you'll get for gifts are different fancy sketchbooks. This one has a smooth red cover, and the paper is really nice. I only use it when I want to draw something for real. And right now I'd rather be focused on drawing than thinking about what Mom and Dad said.

I start with a castle. Which sounds hard to do, but it really isn't. It's just a bunch of straight lines. Then I start to fill in the ground, the bushes and trees. I'm shading the side of a tree when Dad knocks and lets himself in.

"Airi," he says, coming over to crouch down by the bed. "I think we should talk."

"About what?" I ask, like I have no idea what he means.

"Your mother said a little bit about what happened

tonight," he says. "But I'd like to hear it from you."

"What for?" I say. "It was just an accident. I didn't mean to knock the soup over."

"I know, and your mom knows that too." Dad sighs and lowers himself to sit cross-legged. "Your mom has been having a hard time recently."

"I know," I tell him. "I see her more than you do." I'm annoyed. Why is he telling me this? I'm not unobservant. I can tell Mom is sad.

"That's true." He laughs a little, but he doesn't actually sound like he thinks it's funny. "The recent moves have been difficult, especially with Kaori being so little. That's why if I take that job"—I want to throw up at the mention of it; instead I bend my head closer to my drawing—"I'll go alone. I'm not planning on uprooting all of you again."

"She'd be happier if you were here," I say. "I've been trying to help."

"I know you have," Dad says. "But, Airi, what your mom needs right now is for you to behave so she doesn't have to worry about you."

"That's why I was trying to make her laugh," I explain. "I'm trying to show her she doesn't have to worry."

Dad sighs. "I know you mean well, Airi, but that's not the kind of help I'm talking about."

"You want me to shut up and stop causing trouble," I say.

It's basically what every teacher has ever wanted from me. But I'm not used to hearing it from Dad. "I get it."

"Airi, no," Dad says. "That isn't what I mean."

"Well, it's what it sounds like," I say. I scoot out of the lower bunk. "So you should probably go, since I have school tomorrow. I need my sleep to be a good student."

"Airi," Dad says, sounding tired. "Don't backtalk."

"I'm not," I say. "I'm being entirely serious." Which is true, I am serious. But that's because I'm getting mad, not because I actually want to be a good student. They're treating me like I'm a complete monster. I'm not. They just don't get me. No one does. Not even Dad, it turns out. And I'm mad that Mrs. Ashton has been talking to them. I'm mad that I feel like she betrayed me. I have to keep reminding myself that she isn't my friend. She's on the adults' side.

It's a good thing we're doing prank tryouts tomorrow. Because I'm going to need those recruits. I need to show Mrs. Ashton what I'm really capable of. I'm not just a trouble-maker. I'm Trouble. And no one can change that. Not even Dad.

"Fine," Dad says. "But we're going to talk about this again, okay?"

"Yeah, sure." I clamber up the ladder to my bed. "Night, Dad."

Dad sighs again. "Good night, Airi."

He turns off the light when he leaves. I curl up into a ball. Tomorrow can't come soon enough.

SITUATION REPORT

Date
Friday, October 22

Location
Joe Takata Elementary

Activities Planned
The Dare Challenge

Logistical Requirements
Duct tape

Scissors

A mirror

A razor

Habanero chilies

Obstacles Anticipated
Recess monitors

Remarks
If I'm being honest, being able to deal with dares doesn't prove that you'll be any good at pranking. But kids who aren't afraid of dares are also usually brave enough to make trouble. Which is really the key thing here. They don't have to come up with any ideas. They just have to follow my lead. And this will tell me if they have the stomach for that.

25

"LISTEN UP, RECRUITS," I SAY, HANDS ON MY HIPS. "If you want to join the Prank Patrol, you're going to have to prove you can handle it. And to do that, you need to pass three tests."

I hold up my finger. "One: take a piece of duct tape. Put it on the back of your neck. Then one of us"—I gesture to myself and my officers—"will rip it off. Anyone who doesn't scream passes. Ganbatte!"[29]

I see a few kids gulp nervously. Kiana and Grace start passing out pieces of tape. We're gathered in the corner of the blacktop, far enough away that no teachers can see what we're doing. Everyone in Mrs. Ashton's class has asked to

---

29 がんばって (gahn-BAHT-teh) means "Try your best!" If you want to tell someone to "break a leg" before performing on a stage, this is what you'd say. Make sure to pronounce it right.

try out. Which is pretty flattering. I almost want to let all of them join.

But pranking isn't for the weak of heart. You need a strong stomach and absolute bravery. So the tests are necessary.

My recruits grimly slap the tape onto the backs of their necks. Once everyone is taped up, the officers march up and down the rows, ripping the tape off. Neat little squares of bare pinkish skin.

Almost everyone flinches. Some jump away. Natalie instinctively punches Wyatt in the stomach. Only a few make a noise. Only three—Sophia, Gavin, and Brayden—scream. They slump their shoulders when they do. They know they've failed.

"I'm sorry," I say to them. "I appreciate your interest and your willingness to try. We may call on you for assistance, but you are not part of the patrol."

And so the ranks are thinned.

"Next!" I produce a shaving razor I stole from Mom's toiletries. "You must shave a stripe in your eyebrow. It can be either eyebrow, and it can be as big or small as you like. But it must be noticeable, and we *will* be judging on how far you're willing to go."

This gets a little more fear from the recruits. Good. They should be afraid. There is no courage without fear.

One by one our classmates march up to Mei, who has a mirror.

Schwip.

Schwip.

Eyebrow hairs fall to the ground like rain. Most of the kids are pretty cautious about it. But a few go the distance. Chloe gives herself a big diagonal stripe. Andy actually shaves off his entire right eyebrow. By the end, we've got ourselves a proper pirate crew.

No one has disqualified themselves this round. But that's okay, because the last round will be the make-or-break.

I pull out the final test. I reveal it to everyone: a container of sliced habanero peppers.

"These," I say, "are some of the spiciest peppers in the world. Anything spicier than this is basically instant death." I open the lid and let the smell float to them. People's eyes start watering right away. "Each of you will put a slice in your mouth. When you spit it out, it's over. The eight who last the longest are in." I pause, letting them take it in. Everyone is watching me with complete attention. "Use a fork to get it out," I say. "You don't want to accidentally rub your eyes after touching these."

This time the recruits look actively worried. Mei has extra forks she took from the cafeteria to pass around. Aidan says he isn't going to try it because he can't eat spicy food. Kai wants to know why the officers don't have to participate.

"They've proven their loyalty," I say. "I don't need anything else from them."

"I'll do it," Mei says. "On behalf of all of us." She spears a slice of habanero.

"Are you sure?" I whisper. "It really is super spicy."

Mei looks a little pale, but she nods. "Start the challenge."

Jason holds up a flag he made out of a bandanna. I count down. "Three . . . two . . . one . . . go!" Jason drops the flag. Everyone brings their habanero to their mouth.

For a few seconds, everything is quiet. Then, like a magic trick, people start to turn red. A few cough. A single tear runs down Mei's face.

Sawyer is the first to spit his out. Then Sophia. They run to the cafeteria for milk. Others soon follow. Until the only people left are Kai and Mei. Staring each other down. Too stubborn to give up even if they've already made it into the crew. They want to prove who's really the bravest. Mei's hands are balled into fists. Tears are dripping off her chin. Her nose is all snotty. Kai is bright red and shaking. A little bit of drool comes from his mouth.

Mei takes a step forward. Then another. She leans in. Right in Kai's face.

Kai holds on a few seconds more. Then he turns and spits out the slice, gasping. "Ack," he says. His voice is hoarse. "You're nuts, Mei."

Mei stands up straight and delicately spits her slice into a napkin she has clutched in her hand. She looks awful. But she's smiling. Triumphant. Her mouth looks like it's a little blistered. "Even if I weren't already an officer, I'd be in," she tells him. "See? Still want to challenge the rest of us?"

Kai shakes his head. "Semper fi, Mei." He salutes. Then he runs off for milk.

Mei stays standing straight. The rest of us circle her, looking at her nervously. She's looking kind of green.

"Mei?" Kiana asks. "Are you okay?"

"I think," Mei says, "I'm gonna throw up." She pushes her ponytail over her shoulder, walks to the nearest trash can, and hurls into it.

"Wow," Wyatt says. "That's so metal."

I have to agree.

SITUATION REPORT

Date
Monday, October 25,
through Friday, October 29

Location
Joe Takata Elementary

Activities Planned
Preparing the haunted
house

Logistical Requirements
Paint

Fake spiderwebs

LOTS of cardboard

Candy bowl

Music

Will the school let us bring
in a fog machine???

Fake blood

Candy

Obstacles Anticipated
So far Mrs. Ashton and Ms.
Nicole have let us do what
we want, but it's always
possible they might find out
something and decide it's
too much. That's why we're
keeping our best surprises
and scares a secret.

Remarks
This is less of a prank than
a performance, but there
are prank-like bits. Surprises
and jokes for the trick-or-
treaters. Halloween is fun
like that. It's the one time
of year when pranks can be
scary too, because people
are expecting that and a lot
of times they'll laugh about
being scared. Because we
know that mummy isn't
really going to curse us and
that werewolf isn't going to
bite us.

Originally this part of my
plan was to just mess up
the classroom. But I couldn't
figure out a way to do that
and not completely wreck
things, which I don't want.
This is better, because we
completely transform the
room AND make it haunted
since Mrs. Ashton believes
in ghosts. Maybe we'll
even shock her! But the
important part is that she
acknowledges that I'm the
more creative prankster.
The champion. And then
I'll be able to go back to
thinking of her as any other
teacher. Because she'll
realize there's no teaching
me. I am who I am.

26

With our troops readied, it's time to start giving orders. Everyone has a job. Little secrets to hide in our class's haunted house. Mrs. Ashton is impressed with how eager we are to decorate.

"Usually the sixth graders are pretty sick of this," she says. "But if you win us that pizza party, I won't complain!"

Mrs. Ashton helps me with the big butcher-paper mural I'm making of a dungeon. It's going to go on the back wall. Then we'll put spiderwebs over it. She's not bad at painting. She even shows me how to paint the rocks to look more real.

"If you flick the brush like

this, see?" She uses her fingernail to splatter the sheet. Now the rocks look like they have some dirt on them. "Try it."

I do. It looks cool. Although I do get some paint on myself.

Kiana and Grace make a cardboard cutout of an old television. That's gonna be for me. Not that Mrs. Ashton knows that. As far as she knows, we're making the haunted house and then going trick-or-treating along with everyone else. But where's the fun in that?

We spend the entire day of the Halloween party getting the classroom ready. Mrs. Ashton lets us do it on our own since we're sixth graders. She goes to help the other teachers set up the school for when families start arriving.

We turn our classroom into a twisty maze. It's dark and eerie. Glow sticks light the floor. Andy brought speakers for his phone and has it set to creepy haunted-house noises, like creaky doors and loud wind. Kiana is hiding beneath Mrs. Ashton's desk. Every few minutes, she lets out a horrible, terrible scream. Jason is going to be a scarecrow and stand still until someone gets close. Then he'll jump out at them.

We have normal baby haunted-house stuff too. A bowl full of cooked spaghetti labeled "guts." Peeled grapes, or "eyeballs." For extra fun, I mixed together a huge bowl of M&M's and Skittles for people to grab as they leave, along with the fun-size candy bars.

When school ends, we all run to get ready. I've already got practice putting on my creepy little girl costume. So it takes me no time at all. I slick up my hair and powder my face like I've done it a hundred times. Mei puts in fake fangs. Kiana draws stitches on her neck with her mom's eyeliner pencil. We make a ghoulish sight.

I turn and let my hair drape in front of my face. "You're next," I hiss at Mei.

"I vill not be keeled by such a feeble creature," Mei says in a heavy accent.

Then it's time to take our places. I hide behind the cardboard TV cutout with paper we painted with a staticky pattern and turn on my iPod, which I loaded up with the sound of a broken TV. I have to wait until I hear Mei's voice. She's in charge of leading people through the haunted house. She has a whole speech planned.

The first few groups of kids come through. All from the fifth grade. I hear them scream when Jason jumps out at them. Then they scream again when they come to Wyatt, dressed as a zombie, who lurches toward them like he wants to eat them. By the time they get to my area, they're all freaked out. Mei is telling them about the horrible curse that falls on anyone who watches too much TV.

"There's a little girl who watched so much TV that her entire house flooded," Mei says, "and she never stopped watching. She drowned, just like that. Her spirit was trapped in the TV, and now she travels from screen to screen, crawling out to watch with you."

I poke my head through the cardboard TV cutout. I slump over, letting my arms fall limp on the ground. "Must . . . watch . . ." I say in a creaky voice. I claw at the carpet like I'm trying to use it to get myself out of the TV. I look up through my hair at the terrified faces of the fifth graders. The girl with the cat-eye glasses from E.J.'s class is there. I reach for her, my mouth wide open.

"So . . . hungry . . ." I croak. My fingers brush the bottom of her princess dress, and she screams. They all run away toward the exit. They probably think they're safe. Little do they know that Liam is hiding behind the bowl of candy. We put a hole in the bottom and glued a glove to it so the candy doesn't fall out. Then Liam sticks his hand into the glove, and if anyone reaches too deep—BAM! He's got them.

Another few groups come through. I change up my lines a little every time. When a few of the littler kids come in, I smile at them and try not to be quite as scary. They still shriek. I do look pretty horrible.

I'm waiting, though. Waiting for the real prankee. I have a final trick up my sleeve. Literally.

I hear Mrs. Ashton's voice first. She's praising our creativity. She even yelps a few times. I take my secret weapon from my sleeve and pop it in my mouth. Then I start my slow crawl out of the TV.

This time I really give it my all. "I'm so . . . lonely . . ." I moan. "Won't you be my friend?" I reach out for Mrs. Ashton's feet. I grab at her ankle. And as I do, I chomp down hard on the fake-blood capsule in my mouth.

Fake blood gushes from my mouth. I wish I'd had one of these for my James Cook performance. I grab at Mrs. Ashton's leg. "Please . . . help me!" I collapse to the ground.

TRICKS

Mrs. Ashton gasps.

I roll over onto my back, spasming dramatically. I flop around before going still. The last of the fake blood drips from my mouth. I should be an actress. That was Oscar material there.

I wait for applause. For Mrs. Ashton to tell me how creative I am and admit I've won. Instead, I hear a familiar little girl's voice saying, "Mommy!" and then bursting into tears.

I roll over quickly and push myself onto my knees. There's a little girl here too. Eva. It must be. She's got curly black hair and big black eyes. She's dressed as a bumblebee. She's clinging to Mrs. Ashton's hand, trying to hide behind her.

I wipe my mouth and say, "It's okay, it isn't real." I push my hair out of my face. "See?"

But Eva only starts crying harder. When I try to reach out

to her, she shrieks and scuttles away. It's like being punched in the stomach.

"Airi, could you back up?" Mrs. Ashton asks. Her brow is wrinkled. Her glasses are slipping down her nose. She scoops up Eva, who hides her face in Mrs. Ashton's neck. "She won't calm down with you so close."

"But I can help," I say. "I'm good with kids. I can show her that it's all pretend—"

"Not right now, Airi," Mrs. Ashton says firmly. She's never sounded so stern with me before. And I've been expecting it, or I thought I'd been. This moment, where she stops thinking I'm funny and decides I'm just an annoying kid. Where she's disappointed by me. But this isn't like I thought it would be. This time it hurts.

I stand there. Feeling useless. Feeling awful. I'm all covered in fake blood, and I didn't even make Mrs. Ashton laugh. I only made Eva cry. The only thing I'm good at is pranks and causing trouble. That's what everyone's always said. And my number one rule is to make people happy. What good am I if I can't even do that?

I watch as Mrs. Ashton carries Eva out of the room. My stomach is churning like I drank sour milk. I don't want to be in this ridiculous haunted house anymore. So I go. I march out of there and go to sit in front of the school to wait for my parents. Families walk past me. A few ask if I'm okay. I just kick at the asphalt and mentally beg my parents to get there faster.

"Airi?" Dad sounds worried. I look up through my hair. Mom is with Kaori, who's dressed like a pumpkin.

"Hi," I say. "Don't take Kaori to my class." I get up and rub at my face. "Can I go home?"

"But Halloween's your favorite holiday," Dad says.

The thought of candy and costumes normally would perk me right up. But right now the thought of seeing anything related to Halloween makes my chest feel all tight.

I shake my head. "I want to go home."

Dad and Mom look at each other. Dad says, "I'll take her," and Mom nods. She takes Kaori into the school. I hear people cooing about how cute she is. She really is very cute. The cutest pumpkin who ever lived.

Dad tries to get me to talk a few times on the drive home. But I'm not in the mood. Today was supposed to be my triumph. I was supposed to prank Mrs. Ashton so good that she would have to admit that I'm the best. So that she would give her deep laugh that I've heard only once.

It occurs to me that I've changed. Making her laugh wasn't my original plan. I started out trying to make her give up. But she didn't. She never did. She kept trying to be nice to me. And look at what I did. I completely blew it. I made her daughter cry. I ruined Halloween. I bet she won't ever want to see me again. I know I wouldn't.

At home, I take a shower and go to lie down flat on my lower bunk. Dad comes in a few minutes later and approaches my fort. He brings his feet together and straightens up. Perfect military posture. "Permission to enter?"

"Permission not granted," I say. I turn over onto my side.

"Airi," Dad says, "what's wrong? Talk to me."

"What's the point?" I mumble. "You're just going away soon anyway. You can't help."

"I want to talk to you about that, actually." Dad knocks against the bed frame. "Can I come in?"

"I guess," I mutter.

Dad sits down at the end of the bottom bunk. He has to hunch to fit. I curl up in the corner by the wall, hugging my pillow to my chest. I peer at him through my wet hair. He looks tired.

"It's okay," I say. "I know you really love your job. It's not like I want you to quit or anything."

I'm lying. I'd love it if he quit. It would mean he wouldn't get to wear his uniform anymore, and we might have to move houses again, but he'd be home more. But if I tell him it's okay, maybe he'll leave me alone. I'm not going to be a problem. Not for him. I'm already a problem for Mom and for Mrs. Ashton. I can't be a problem for him too.

"Why do you think I joined the army, Airi?" Dad asks.

It's not what I'm expecting him to ask. I turn over onto my back and narrow my eyes at him. "Because of Great-Grandpa."

"Partially. But also because they paid for me to go to college." Dad looks thoughtful. "I'm proud to have served. I don't always agree with everything we do. There's a lot I disagree with, actually. But I keep doing my job because it gets food and supplies to soldiers around the world. It's important."

"I know," I say. "It's more important than us."

"No, Airi, that isn't what I'm saying." Dad hunches in more. "But it *is* an obligation and a pledge that I have to honor."

"You made a pledge to us too," I say. "And to Mom. But you never think about that. You just move us around, and then you leave for ages. You never think about what happens to us when you're gone. And sometimes we don't even know where you're going or if you're going to come back—" I start crying. Which I hate. I shove my pillow into my face.

"Airi—"

"No!" I sit up and throw the pillow at him. It bounces off his face. "You *promised.* You said that you'd stay. That this would be better and you'd be around more, but you *lied.* And it makes Mom sad, and it makes E.J. sad, and I don't know how to make it better! Every time I try I just mess everything up." I clench my jaw. "So get out. I don't want to talk to a liar."

Dad just nods. Which is as good as admitting that I'm right. He leaves without even saying goodbye. He closes the door behind him. And as soon as he does, I start crying again. And this time I don't stop for a long time.

AFTER ACTION REPORT

Date
Friday, October 29

Location
Joe Takata Elementary

Actions Undertaken
Haunted house

Duration
One hour?

Purpose
Some fun scares

Mission Result
Technically we were very successful, but it doesn't feel like it.

Remarks
I guess this means I won the prank war. But Mrs. Ashton won't want anything to do with me now. I wouldn't want to have anything to do with me either. I did succeed in proving that she's like every other teacher. They all give up eventually. It's just that I was starting to think I was wrong. Usually I hate being wrong, but I think this time I would have been okay with it. But I was right.

I'M NOT GOiNG TO SCHOOL ANYMORE. I'VE DECiDED.
It's clearly not the place for me.

I tell Mom this when she comes to find out where I am on Monday. I've been in my room all weekend. I didn't even come out for meals. Or even actual Halloween. Instead I snuck downstairs in the night and raided the fridge. I have a lot of trash in my room. But I don't want to talk to anyone. The thought of it makes me want to barf. Just talking to Mom now has my stomach churning with remembered guilt. If I saw Mrs. Ashton, I would actually barf.

"You have to go to school," Mom says.

"I'm sick," I tell her. "I'm having a Bad Day." I don't think this is exactly what happens to her. But I'm hoping she'll understand.

Mom hesitates. Then she says, "I'll call the school."

I'm too tired to wonder why she gave in. It's for the best. I'm sure Mrs. Ashton doesn't want me in class either.

I tell Mom the same thing the next day. And the next. She keeps letting me stay home. Which makes no sense, because normally Mom makes me go to school even if I have a 99.9-degree fever. If it isn't over 100, it doesn't count.

By Thursday I'm sick of my room. I lie outside in the backyard instead, watching the clouds move. When I finally drag myself back to my room, I'm all warm and ready to sleep again. But when I open my door, I discover something strange.

The floor of my bedroom, from the door to my desk, is covered in plastic cups. And each plastic cup has water in it. There's no way to get to my bed except to take every single one to the sink to dump out. Or knock them all over.

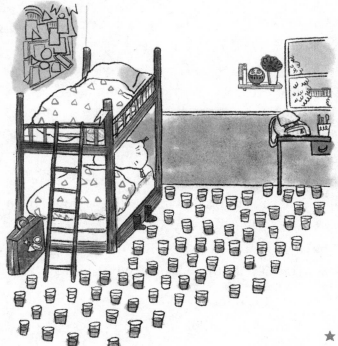

I turn around and go down to E.J.'s room to yell at him. But he isn't in there. And when I touch the doorknob, my hand gets sticky. Someone put jam on it.

I stare at my jammed hand. Despite myself, I'm starting to smile. These are actually pretty good pranks. It must be Dad trying to make me feel better. And I do, a little, even if I'm not ready to forgive him just yet.

I go downstairs to find him. When I reach the bottom of the staircase and turn the corner, I'm hit in the face with Silly String. I bat it away from my face and see Mom standing there, lips pressed together. Except she doesn't look mad. She looks . . . like she's trying not to laugh.

"Mom?" I ask. She sprays me in the face again. I sputter and flail. I hear a strange sound. A laugh. One I haven't heard in a long time.

Mom is laughing. At me. But not *at* me.

"Mom!" I try to steal the can from her hand. "Who are you? What have you done with my mom?"

"Is this helping you cheer up?" Mom asks. She sprays me in the face again. I'm draped in Silly String now. "Because there's someone here to see you."

"You're so weird," I tell her. But I'm grinning. I've never seen Mom be silly like this. I like it. "Who's here?"

Mom points to the kitchen. She gives me one last spray as I walk past. I hear her giggling as I step inside and see Mrs. Ashton sitting at our table, sipping a cup of tea.

"Oh," I say. My good mood is gone. "Hi."

"Hello, Airi," Mrs. Ashton says. She smiles. "Your mom and I have been having some fun."

"You have?"

"I told you I was a champion prankster," Mrs. Ashton says, smiling wider.

I sit down across from her and drop my head to the table. "I'm not. I thought I was, but all I do is make people upset."

"I don't know about that," Mrs. Ashton says. "Your haunted house won our class the pizza party. It's happening tomorrow. I'd really like it if you were there."

"I don't deserve it," I tell the table. "I made Eva cry."

"You did," Mrs. Ashton agrees. "That wasn't great. But sometimes we make mistakes. But when we make mistakes, we don't just give up. We pick ourselves up and try again."

I look at her. "I ruined your class," I say. "I made everyone work against you. Why don't you hate me?"

"Always so to the point," Mrs. Ashton says. "That's one of the things I like about you." She sips her tea, then puts the mug down. She's using my favorite one, the one with dinosaurs that appear when there's hot water inside. "I told you, Airi. I used to be a lot like you. I didn't like school. I played a lot of pranks. I was very unhappy for a very long time. I want to make school a place you like coming to, because you're a very bright girl."

"I can't even read," I say.

"You're dyslexic," Mrs. Ashton says. "That's all."

I sit up straight. "Diss-what?"

"Dyslexic," Mrs. Ashton says. "From the word 'dyslexia.' It means that you have trouble with letters and words. It's fairly common. It doesn't mean that you're stupid or that you can't learn to love reading. Your brain just works a little differently, that's all. And I would like to keep working with you to find strategies for learning that suit your abilities."

"Like picture math," I say.

"Like picture math," Mrs. Ashton agrees.

I didn't know there was a word for people like me. People who couldn't just look at words and have them make sense. I form the word in my mouth. I like the way it feels. I try applying it to me. I'm dyslexic. Airi Sano is dyslexic. It actually sounds kind of cool.

"I'm not going to make it easy on you," I tell her.

"I know," she says. "But can you prom-ise me that you'll try?" She holds out her hand. I take it. We shake.

"And," Mrs. Ashton says, "if you come back to school tomorrow, I have a great idea for a joke we can play on the rest of the class."

I perk up right

away. "I'm listening," I say. So she tells me. And I have to say, it's a pretty awesome idea.

Mrs. Ashton and I talk a little while longer before she leaves. She even video calls Eva to show me that Eva is doing okay. I tell Eva I'm sorry for scaring her, but she doesn't even seem to remember it happening. Which I guess is how little kids are.

After Mrs. Ashton leaves, I look for Mom. She's folding laundry, humming to herself. She seems happy. I almost don't go in. But then I think about her laughter. And how much I missed it.

"Mom," I say. She turns to look at me. "I'm sorry."

Mom holds out her arms. I run to her and hug her tight. She rubs my back. "I'm sorry too, Airi," she says. "I was so stressed that I didn't notice you felt the same way. I should know by now that you don't do things like everyone else." She lets go and holds me at arm's length. "Dad told me that you've been trying to cheer me up. Is that true?"

I shrug. "I guess."

"Oh, Airi." She hugs me again. "I'm always going to be sad sometimes. But it isn't your job to fix it." She squeezes me tight. "You still better start helping me more around the house. No more messing with dinner."

I laugh. "Okay," I say. "I promise."

"Now let's go clean up the cups in your room," Mom says. "That one was Hattie's idea. We need to pick them up before Mr. Knuckles knocks them over."

By the time Dad gets home, we're making dinner to-gether. E.J. has come back from his friend's house, where they were studying. He hasn't said anything more about pri-vate school. I need to tell him that it's okay if he goes. I still don't want him to skip a grade, though. That would be so embarrassing.

Dad gives me a big hug when he sees that I'm out of my room. "Glad to have you back," he says. He kisses the top of my head. I hug him back. I have to get my hugs in while I can.

We eat spaghetti and meatballs for dinner. One of my favorites. Mom's too. Though she says it tastes different in Japan. Things feel okay for once. Like we're not all about to start arguing at any second. It's almost peaceful, except for Kaori throwing noodles into E.J.'s hair.

"I have news," Dad tells us when we're finishing up. All of us pause. I can tell that we're all worried. But Dad is smiling. Smiling real big. "I'm not being sent to Guam."

Mom drops her fork. "What?"

"Oh my god!" I yell. I run around the table and fling my-self into his arms. Dad catches me, laughing.

"How?" Mom asks.

"I advised my superiors that while I'm honored, my cur-rent priority is my family." Dad squeezes me. "And they said they'd have me review training materials from here instead."

I shriek in delight. Kaori echoes me. I jump up and pull Kaori out of her seat to dance around the room. Even E.J. is grinning. He gets up to hug Dad too. Mom has her hand to her mouth. Her eyes are a little wet, like she's crying. But this time it's because she's happy.

"I still have a few more years before retirement," Dad says. "But I'm going to do everything I can to keep us together until then. Airi, you were right. I wasn't thinking about how hard this has been for you."

I clutch Kaori to my chest. "It's your job."

"I do have some say in what I do." Dad gets up, E.J. clinging to his back like a monkey. "I haven't tried to swing my weight around before. I never thought it was right. But this is worth it. You're worth it." He reaches back and pulls E.J. off, tickling him in the sides until E.J. collapses to the floor.

Mom gets up and hugs Dad. Then they start to kiss, and I cover my and Kaori's eyes. "Gross," I tell them.

Dad is laughing again. It's still the best sound in the entire world. "You guys can go. Mom and I will take care of the dishes."

"It's because they want to kiss more," I tell Kaori. She babbles happily and smacks me in the nose.

It's only when E.J. goes to his room and yells, "Is this jam?" that Mom and I remember we forgot to clean that up. We look at each other. Mom bites her lip and lifts her hand to hide her laughter. It's nice to be on her team.

INCIDENT REPORT

Date
Thursday, November 4

Location
Fort Shafter, Hawai'i

Event Description
Mom wants to prank Dad. She doesn't really get the concept of it yet—her first idea was to change the station his car radio is set to. Which is okay, it's just really easy for him to change it back. She hasn't learned how to take it that one step further, which is doing it every day. And for maximum impact, a different station every time.

She seems nervous about it, though. Which is cute. It's the most harmless prank I've ever heard. Dad probably won't even realize it's a prank for a few days. But I'm going to help her do it. And then when Dad eventually comes home one day complaining about his car radio being broken, I can't wait to see her try to keep a straight face. I bet she can't.

I MAKE MY TRiUMPHANT RETURN TO CLASS ON FRiDAY by striding in and proclaiming, "I am back!"

Mei rolls her eyes and says, "We can see that." But it's okay, because she and everyone else start talking about how epic the haunted house was. Even if I left. I listen to everything they tell me. It sounds like they had a lot of fun. After I left, Mei took over the haunted TV. Apparently she was so scary she made the principal scream. I wish I could have seen that.

Right before lunch, Mrs. Ashton sends me to the office to pick up the pizzas. She winks at me as I go. I wink back.

I bring the pizza boxes to class and set them down on Mrs. Ashton's desk. "Bon appétit, everyone!" I say. I fling open the top box.

Inside is a veggie tray. Cucumber, carrots, broccoli, ranch.

Everyone looks around in confusion. I pick up a carrot, dip it in the ranch, and take a big bite. "Mmm," I say. "I just love fresh vegetables."

"Me too," Mrs. Ashton says. She takes a slice of cucumber. "Very refreshing, don't you think?"

She grins at me. I take another carrot. I look around at everyone. "Aren't you gonna eat some?" I ask. "We worked so hard for it."

"What happened to the pizza?" Liam asks.

Mrs. Ashton frowns. "Pizza? Who said anything about pizza?"

I can hardly hold back my laughter as everyone starts whispering, trying to figure out if they all heard wrong. Or if it was a rumor or a joke. I wait until most of them are turned away to remove the top box and open the next one. I inhale the smell of cheese and pepperoni. Mrs. Ashton and I take the first pieces and cheers.

"Hey!" Kiana catches on. "There *is* pizza!"

"Oops," I say to Mrs. Ashton.

"They figured us out," she says.

Everyone crowds around the desk, jostling to get their pieces. I move to stand next to Mrs. Ashton's chair. Everyone is laughing and smiling. Saying they knew we were lying. That they didn't fall for it. I know better.

Jason dips his pizza in the ranch from the veggie tray. Which is so gross. I'm glad he's my friend. Mei picks all the onions off her veggie piece. Wyatt eats two pieces so fast I'm sure he's going to make himself sick.

I feel proud. I feel like I've just climbed a mountain and shouted out to hear my echo. I've never had this before. A group of friends. A place where I feel like I belong. We spent so long moving, I thought I'd never have it. But now I have a chance to start again. To make this place a real home.

I can't wait.

PERSONNEL FILE

Name
Ashton, Harriet, aka Hattie

Date of Birth
April 5 (I asked her!)

Place of Birth
Spokane, Washington

Place of Residence
Pearl City, Hawai'i

Occupation
Sixth-grade teacher

Primary Specialties
Pranks, teaching new ideas, speaking very softly

Awards and Citations
Best Prankster

Disciplinary Record
She told me about one time she played a prank that ended with her sister's friend getting singed eyebrows. She got grounded for two weeks for that.

Remarks
I don't know if Mrs. Ashton is "cool." But she is special. She's a good teacher. The first one to really try to understand me. The first one who didn't give up. I didn't make it easy. On her or my other teachers. I wanted them to give up.

Her wife brought Eva to the school the other day so Eva could meet me for real.

I apologized for scaring her, and she showed me how good she is at whistling now. Mrs. Ashton's wife is nice too. She's an engineer for the city of Honolulu, which she says means she builds things. Her name is Melissa.

Mrs. Ashton has given me some more tests for my dyslexia so we understand how it works. She explained to me how my brain works different. How other people see words not as a jumble of shapes but as parts. I don't know if I'll ever get there. But it's nice to know.

I think I'm excited about school. Which is gross. I don't want to be E.J. But school always felt like banging my head on a wall. Now it feels like a big open field. Or a museum with lots to see. I'll have to figure this out as I go.

PERSONNEL FILE

Name
Sano, Airi

Date of Birth
April 7

Place of Birth
Sagamihara, Japan

Place of Residence
Fort Shafter, Hawai'i

Occupation
Prankmaster General

Primary Specialties
Causing trouble, making people laugh, pranks

Awards and Citations
Most Disruptive Student, Best Baby Soother, Prankster Extraordinaire

Disciplinary Record
Too long to include full list

Remarks
I've been getting better grades at school. Ones that I'm proud to show Mom and Dad. I got an A on an essay, and Mom nearly cried. I worked really hard on it. Which was tiring. Don't know if I'll do that again. There's nothing wrong with a B. But it's nice to feel like I get things.

Dad and I made a deal. He'll sign me up for karate lessons if I bring my grades up to a B average for the first semester. I told him that grades are a shallow way to judge whether someone has actually learned. But honestly Mrs. Ashton grades pretty fairly on that. She doesn't mark me down for spelling or bad handwriting.

Anyway, I shouldn't have said that. Because now he says that at Christmas, I'm going to have to explain, in detail, to Grandma and Grandpa what I learned this year. I think this is more of a punishment than anything. But I do really want to learn karate. And Jason said he'll sign up too. Now we just have to convince Mei and some others and I'll have my own pirate crew. And then? Who knows what we'll do.

Acknowledgments

The first time I met Airi Sano, I was a fresh college graduate working as an intern for the earliest incarnation of Cake Creative Kitchen. To be here almost a decade later as the person trusted to bring Airi and her story to life is beyond surreal. I owe deep thanks to Dhonielle Clayton, whose unwavering faith in passing Airi to me has changed my life, as well as to all past and present members of Cake Creative. I am in awe of Jennifer Naalchigar, whose art brought Airi and her friends to life and who at some points seemed like she was peering directly into my brain for references—I can't wait for everyone to see what you've done.

Getting this book to print took the work and support of many. Thanks go to my writing group, Pug Squad, for always being there as both fellow creatives and supportive friends; Cake Creative editors Annie Nybo and Kate Sullivan; Clay Morrell, also of Cake Creative; and of course our agent, Suzie Townsend, and her team, as well as my fantastic editor, Talia Benamy, and everyone at Philomel. (Special shoutout to the production team—I know what you go through.)

I won't pretend to be an authority on the Japanese American experience. Everyone's story is different; mine was shaped by my grandparents' Christmas tree farm and vacations spent on the windward side of O'ahu with my family. Thank you to Aunty Evelyn, Cathy, Cassie, and my mom for answering my questions about living and growing up in Hawai'i, and to Chad and Kei, as well as our authenticity reader, Akiko Sekihata, for providing guidance on aspects of Japanese language and culture. Airi's view of Hawaiian and Japanese culture is one based on my own experiences; I encourage any readers who are interested in learning more to look for works by authors native to those cultures.

Lastly, I owe deep thanks to my incredible network of support, starting with my parents, who have indulged my little writing habit for decades; my Mira Costa (and MBMS and Pennekamp) friends—Sara, you may recognize some games we used to play; my New York family, from the Building Inspectors to Sasha and Maggie, who have seen me at my absolute worst and love me anyway, to Alyssa, who remains my biggest hype person; the people at Emerson College who shaped my writing, both my classmates and my professors, especially my thesis advisors, Mako Yoshikawa and Rick Reiken; and to everyone who told me they were excited to read this book. Among all the weirdness and uncertainty of the world since March 2020, you all have kept me sane and whole.

Author's Land Acknowledgments

I am the descendant of Japanese immigrants to Hawai'i. I acknowledge Hawai'i as an Indigenous space where the descendants of the original people are Kānaka Maoli. I recognize that her majesty Queen Lili'uokalani yielded the Hawaiian Kingdom and these territories under duress and protest to the United States to avoid the bloodshed of her people. I further recognize that generations of Indigenous Hawaiians and their knowledge systems shaped Hawai'i in a sustainable way that allows us to enjoy her gifts today. For this, I am grateful, and I seek to support the Kānaka Maoli in their efforts to protect their land and communities.

Photo by Sara Ford

ZOE TOKUSHIGE originally hails from Southern California but has spent the past decade on the East Coast. After attending NYU for a BS in media, culture, and communication, Zoe received an MFA in creative writing from Emerson College before returning to New York to work in publishing. Zoe currently works at Penguin Random House. When not writing, Zoe enjoys crafts, video games, and D&D.

You can visit Zoe Tokushige online at ZoeTokushige.com and follow her on Twitter and Instagram @ZoeTokushige.

JENNIFER NAALCHIGAR is a British Japanese illustrator based in Hertfordshire, England. She has a love for quirky characters and enjoys experimenting with digital brushes. Jennifer can often be found listening to music and doodling with her tablet in a coffee shop. She also enjoys reading picture books to her kids and scanning anything she can get her hands on. After five years working as an art buyer for Oxford University Press, she decided that illustration was the career for her.

You can follow Jennifer on Instagram @NaalchiDraws.